# Recollection and Retribution

# Michael Anderson

Copyright © 2023 Michael Anderson

www.michaelanderson.org

Published by JMHA Publishing

The right of Michael Anderson to be identified as the author of this work has been asserted by Michael Anderson in accordance with the Copyright, Designs and Patents Act 1988.

All rights reserved. This book is copyright material and must not be copied, stored, distributed, transmitted, reproduced or otherwise made available in any form, or by any means (electronic, digital, optical mechanical, photocopying, recording or otherwise) without the prior written permission of the publisher.

This is a work of fiction. Names, characters, business, events and incidents are the products of the author's imagination. Any resemblance to actual persons, living or dead, or actual events is purely coincidental.

ISBN : 979-8-3947714-2-2

**Books by Michael Anderson**

*SHORT STORY COLLECTIONS*

Gardening by Moonlight
Nighthawks
Twelve
Live Long and Prosper

*NOVELS*

Heaven's Above
The Return of Magic
Not Where But When
Section O
Old Gods
Heaven's Above, Three Years On
Recollection and Retribution

*POETRY*

Aus meinen Fingern gesogen
(in German)

## DEDICATION

To whom else but Jane Austen, that extraordinary writer whose mercilessly observant eye brought to life the people and mores of her world, encapsulating a certain time and place and the behaviour of its various classes, to the extent that it is now quite impossible to think of Regency England without thinking of her. And let us not forget she has also managed the nigh–impossible feat of her writing being as popular today as it ever was over two centuries ago.

In doing background research for this book I was overwhelmed by the unexpectedly seemingly endless number of websites dedicated to every aspect and minutiae of Jane Austen herself and the associated Regency period in which she lived, from balls to parasols to dresses to breakfasts and bonnets and analyses of her books.

While I have taken my inspiration from this literary giant's place and time, I sincerely hope I have produced something that is much more than a simple pastiche, and rather a story that stands up in its own right, not only set in her world but as something Jane Austen might herself have enjoyed reading. As I sincerely hope you will.

Michael Anderson
London, 2023

## CONTENTS

| | |
|---|---|
| Acknowledgments | i |
| Chapter I | 1 |
| Chapter II | 17 |
| Chapter III | 27 |
| Chapter IV | 39 |
| Chapter V | 49 |
| Chapter VI | 57 |
| Chapter VII | 67 |
| Chapter VIII | 83 |
| Chapter IX | 95 |
| Chapter X | 105 |
| Chapter XI | 117 |
| Chapter XII | 129 |
| Chapter XIII | 139 |
| Chapter XIV | 155 |
| Dramatis Personae | 163 |
| Places & Things | 165 |
| About the Author | 167 |

# Acknowledgments

As ever, the love and support of my wife Karen contributed immensely to the creation of this book. The cover image is by Photowitch.

# 1

THE FIRST TIME Kitty laid eyes upon him she was sitting at her favourite window seat, bathed in the warm glow of a golden sun sinking to the horizon against a flawless sky of Wedgewood blue. Later she was quite unable to recall which novel she had just finished and laid to one side.

The inability to summon up even a vestigial memory of its contents was, she thought, the most damning criticism possible. For what literary work of any merit whatsoever, once read from beginning to end, does not leave the reader in thoughtful re-examination of at least some of its passages and themes? Cause us to essay a doomed attempt to cling on, immersed and unwilling to finally depart the shores of the world conjured up by the author, and thereby return to the mundanity of the everyday?

All she could remember was that it had a particularly fine cover of intricate gold leaf, and she reflected that as with so many things in life, a splendid exterior was no reliable guide at all to the merits of the interior, a thought she was to recall in the future in light of subsequent events.

She looked up from her reverie and saw a carriage enter the distant gates. It inexplicably came to a halt a short way along the drive, and she watched with idle curiosity as a man in a travelling cloak descended and stood motionless in the driveway, apparently studying Longton Manor, her home.

After a moment or two he reboarded the carriage. It jolted into motion and moments later drew up at the front door where he descended and was greeted by Jackson, fussily directing a footman as he wrestled with a surprisingly large number of battered chests and valises.

He glanced upwards and Kitty saw a man she judged to be in the vicinity of thirty years of age or possibly less with even features and thick unruly brown hair, clean shaven with sun–bronzed skin. He disappeared from view and Kitty, her curiosity aroused, made her way downstairs, taking some care to avoid any appearance of unseemly haste. Who could he be?

Upon entering the drawing room she saw her Papa clap the stranger heartily upon his upper arms, and her curiosity grew. Sir Joshua Strickland, *Bart.*, was inordinately proud of that four–letter appendage, granted to some unremarkable ancestor for some forgotten service at some forgotten point after the Restoration. He was both a large man and the gentlest of men, whose love for his family was writ large in his every expression and action.

Notwithstanding his genial nature he could nonetheless appear quite unintentionally formal in manner, so this display of affection and physical contact was sufficiently notable to merit comment.

'Kitty, my dear! Come here, come here and meet your cousin James! James, this is Kitty, the youngest of my three angels!'

'I am delighted to meet you,' said James, 'Sir Joshua is indeed blessed to be surrounded by such beauty.'

He waved casually in a way that somehow encompassed the whole of Longton Manor and the tasteful eau–de–nil drawing room as well as Kitty, who, while her initial impression found both his appearance and voice to be not at all unpleasing, was somewhat less enamoured of being included in the general decor. She performed a perfunctory curtsey and directed her gaze at her beaming father.

'How is it, Papa, that I know nothing of this new cousin? Nor why we were unaware of his arrival?'

Her father gestured for them to sit down and seated himself in his favourite armchair, precisely moulded to the contours of his person by countless seatings over the years. At that moment his two older daughters hurried into the room, managing to wedge themselves inelegantly in the doorway due to her middle sister Alice's impetuous eagerness to be first, leaving the eldest pink–cheeked with embarrassment once disentangled.

'James, allow me to present my two older children, Alice and Olivia. I hope you will forgive their precipitate entrance as I fear that on this occasion curiosity has overcome decorum.'

'There is nothing to forgive, dear Uncle, it was a charmingly impromptu entrance, and it is a singular pleasure to make the acquaintance of three such lovely young ladies in a single day!'

He bowed courteously and seated himself next to Kitty on a sofa, while her older siblings settled themselves upon another. There was a brief pause as all present took the opportunity to examine the newcomer whilst he unabashedly (and rather boldly, thought Kitty) openly returned the favour. For a fleeting moment Kitty supposed that his eyes had lingered upon her a fraction longer than propriety would deem usual, but then her father began speaking and she decided she must have been mistaken.

'My dears,' Sir Joshua began, leaning forward and beaming, 'I am certain you will recollect me speaking to you from time to time about my younger brother Alexander, who joined the East India Company and set off for the Orient not long after I came down from Cambridge. And I believe I recall mentioning the unfortunately rare letters I received from him.'

'Well James here is … was … Alexander's … what should I call you, James? His ward? His stepson perhaps? Forgive me if I take a moment to explain the situation further to my daughters.'

'You see, my angels, my brother Alexander was married to the most charming of women, and she had a sister, and James here is that sister's only son.' The confusion on their faces made him smile but he felt it would be better to expand on James' background when not in his presence.

'Let that suffice for now, my dears, and I will explain further later. James wrote to me informing me of my brother's passing, and of his plans to return to England. I subsequently received his letter with details of his arrival and decided to allow him to surprise you! And there you have it.'

'So, James, it only remains for me to welcome you

to our family home. It is and will remain your home as well for as long as you wish.'

Ignoring the excited agitation of her sister Alice, Kitty turned to James.

'So, Cousin James – for we have to call you something, do we not? So it may as well be "cousin" until one of us comes up with a more specific definition of you, don't you think? So tell us Cousin, have you now put the East behind you for good? And if that is indeed the case, what plans do you have now that you are back in England?'

James smiled and Kitty found herself smiling back as he made himself comfortable against the sofa cushions before replying. There was a certain lack of formality in his manner, in the way he tended to sprawl rather than sit and expressively used his hands to accompany his speech, which Kitty attributed to the unconventional upbringing she vaguely imagined he would have had in India.

'All excellent questions, my dear cousin – how extraordinary to say that for the first time at our ages, and as you say, an excellent catch–all word for want of a better one! Allow me to answer them in the order asked. Yes, since my dear Papa – for that is how I addressed him and how I thought of him – passed away I have severed all my ties to India. I have sold off our house and land, my interest in our trading enterprises, my horse and most of my furniture and chattels. Whatever little remains that I have brought with me is mostly of a personal and sentimental nature.'

'And as to my plans ... now that is a *much* more difficult question! Sir Joshua has been so extraordinarily kind as to welcome me and throw open your home to me, and in order not to outstay my welcome my first order of business must therefore be to find and purchase a home of my own. Only once I am properly settled will I address the matter of what, as they say, to *do*. I do hope that tells you everything you wish to know?'

Kitty knew her questions had been somewhat impertinent, and it was to his credit that he had not only not taken offence but had also responded openly and in such detail. She nonetheless could not help but sense an undertone of mockery in his response and to her intense irritation felt a flush she was certain had made her cheeks go pink. She was however rescued from any embarrassment real or imagined when her mother swept into the room with arms extended and headed for James, much as an advancing army charges inexorably forward to engage its objective.

'My dear, *dear* boy, how wonderful to meet you at last, after so many years of the merest dribs and drabs of news about you and dear Alexander!' she said, leaving his tanned cheek oddly and rakishly adorned with faint streaks of white powder and rouge.

'Oh my, how foolish I am, I suppose I should not call you a boy, should I! Sir Joshua and I were of course *devastated* to hear of dear Alexander's untimely demise and the horror of that news and the concomitant fraternal loss for my poor husband is only now to a small degree salved and alleviated by the present joy of welcoming you into the bosom of your family.'

'Jackson? *Jackson?* Is that you lurking out there? Have I not told you on more than one occasion how I *abhor* lurking? On the other hand it *does* have the virtue of saving me the bother of ringing the bell to summon you, so perhaps on this occasion … '

She seemed to lose her grip on the thread of her thought process as she contemplated her dilemma and took a moment to collect herself before continuing.

'What was I saying … oh yes, kindly ask Mrs Thrupp to … '

She stopped abruptly as the housekeeper appeared behind Jackson and stood before her, hands clasped and as expressionlessly inscrutable as ever. She was a small, wiry and severe woman of indeterminate age dressed from head to toe in unrelieved plain grey with an old-fashioned double ruffle day cap of matching colour, brightened only by an inexplicably jaunty tartan trim, shocking in its gaudy unexpectedness. Kitty had once asked her about it and her reply had been characteristically dour and to the point.

'That is for me to know, and is no business of yours, child. Curiosity killed the cat, you know, so let that be an end to the matter.'

Mrs Thrupp was an immovable rock when she did not wish to answer a question, and the family had all learned the futility of attempting to exert an employer's authority over her to demand she comply. She had been at Longton Manor since in his father's day when Sir Joshua was a boy, since Lady Cecilia arrived as his bride and had been a fixture throughout all three of their daughter's lives, during all of which time none in the family had ever seen her smile.

Her very greyness and infallible competence made her almost invisible as so little input was required from Lady Cecilia and she kept the house (which while not a *great* house was nonetheless a rather *large* house) working so smoothly that this nigh-invisibility went generally unremarked and her eccentricity was simply accepted as the price to pay for that frictionless domesticity.

'Oh! Mrs Thrupp! Really! Must I speak to you as well as Jackson on the irritating nature of lurking? Although I seem to remember I just moderated my opinion somewhat ... now where was I? Oh yes, I recall, kindly prepare and take our guest to the Eastern Room. Oh! Eastern! How amusing, and how appropriate! I had not thought of it until this very moment! What's that you say? All is ready to receive him? Excellent.'

'You must be exhausted, off you go, dear James,' she said, turning to the new arrival. Do take some time to rest and recompose yourself for dinner! We dine punctually at seven, and Jackson will strike the gong in the hall ten minutes beforehand. You cannot fail to hear it no matter where you are in the house. It is Chinese, you know. It is also very old, large and extremely loud. It was a gift from a Mandarin – how exotic that sounds – in Shanghai to Sir Joshua's grandfather. '

With a courtly bow, James allowed himself to be ushered out of the room by Jackson. No sooner was he out of earshot than Sir Joshua faced a determined barrage of questions from his daughters.

'My dear young ladies, let us maintain a modicum of decorum please!' he said, patting the air placatingly. 'Allow me to speak and I shall endeavour to satisfy this unseemly curiosity. There, that's better.'

Even Lady Cecilia had leaned forward apparently agog for his explication, despite being intimately privy to every scrap of information in her husband's possession. Sadly, however, the retention of facts had never been her forte, a quality that might well have constituted a source of irritation for some spouses.

Sir Joshua, however, saw it as a great blessing and source of satisfaction and pleasure, as it allowed him the opportunity to repeatedly revisit any favourite anecdote or interesting item of news and to relate it once more with additional whimsical flourishes and variations like a proud collector burnishing a valued family heirloom, having learned by experience to finely judge the passage of time necessary for its previous expression to have fled his wife's consciousness.

Seeing that he now had their full attention, his fleshy face broke into a fond smile as he surveyed the four females of his household that constituted his universe, the four satellites circling his planet and the care of whose orbits was his fundamental *raison d'être*. The beginnings of frowns of impatience brought him back to the matter at hand and he hastily began speaking.

'Well, my dears, as you know, my brother Alexander joined the East India Company and travelled to Hindustan with his young ward, James. What you may not recall is that his wife, the kindest and most unassuming sister–in–law any man could ever have, had a married sister with one child, namely James. He was still a very small boy when both his parents were killed when the coach in which they were travelling collided with another and plunged off the road down a ravine killing them and one other passenger, with several more injured. A terrible tragedy that left poor James, who was in their Chelsea home with a nanny at the time, as an orphan.'

'My dear brother Alexander and his wife had not

been blessed with children and so they took him in and from that moment on treated him as if he was their own. Unfortunately their pleasure in the child's presence was to her a constant reminder of the horrible and untimely death of her sister, and her inconsolable grief took its toll on her health and it was not long before she too passed away.'

'After that second tragedy, where once there had been five they were now just two, Alexander and his sister–in–law's child James. He had been deeply in love with her, just as I am with your dear Mama, and he was unable to bear continuing to inhabit the places he had shared with her, as each reminded him of his terrible loss.'

'He was fortunate enough to have sufficient funds to allow him to buy his way into the Company, and so off the two of them went, man and boy. I never saw Alexander again and while we did correspond sporadically over the years, he was not a great epistolarian and such communications were few and far between. And then nearly two years ago he died of cholera, a most ghastly disease of the East from which we in these islands have so far been mercifully spared. James had joined his father's business at a young age and it was a lengthy task to arrange matters and liquidate his father's estate, having made the decision to return to us for good. Even though he is not strictly a blood relative, my brother loved him as his own son, and so he is to me, not different in any degree of affection had he been the natural son of my brother, who left him everything he possessed. He is therefore for all intents and purposes my nephew in every way that has meaning. He is to be treated as our closest living relation and is very dear to me for the happiness and companionship he brought Alexander, and our home will be his home until such time as he has found his feet and wishes to seek one of his own. And that is as much as I know.'

He sat back and observed his family, his favourite pastime when not diligently perusing the Times from cover to cover. His eyes rested on Kitty, intelligent, unpredictable and wilful, her dark brown hair a profuse mass of curls and ringlets thicker and more unruly than the general fashion allowed. And while he admitted of no favourites amongst his progeny, there was no denying that she surprised him and lifted his spirits and made him smile not just with greater frequency but in an easy and natural manner that, sadly, Alice and Olivia could not.

As she watched her two sisters chattering excitedly like two fluttering songbirds, both she and her father were quite unaware of having exactly the same indulgent thought, given outward expression by identical affectionate smiles. Alice was the middle daughter, three years older than Kitty, and with blue eyes, perfectly coiffed golden ringlets and a milk–white complexion that made her the very epitome of what in common parlance is termed 'an English Rose.'

She was rhapsodising about their cousin James – his dashing figure, his courtly manners, his exotically sunburned skin, his square jaw – when she was rudely interrupted by her mother.

'Enough, Alice! I do believe you have said all that need be said about our visitor, and I dare say rather more than necessary!'

Lady Cecilia turned to Olivia, who had been silent during Alice's gushing monologue, and tapped her sharply on the arm with a folded fan produced from the tapestry bag that accompanied her everywhere other than to the most formal of balls.

'So tell me, my child, what do *you* think of your long–lost almost–cousin? Do you too find him to your liking?'

'Why, yes, Mama, I do believe so! He is personable, though he can seem odd at times … and *is* quite handsome.'

Kitty remained silent as in her mind's eye she saw the family's future unfold before her with startling clarity. Whatever burgeoning interest James might have awakened in her, something she was quite unready to admit to herself, she was comfortably certain that someone like him – and she suspected him to be a good man with many excellent qualities, although upon what *precisely* this conviction was based eluded her – could not possibly have any interest in a young woman such as Annie, however pretty, who disliked reading, knew little of the world and cared less, and whose life encompassed nothing beyond family, fashion, balls and local gossip.

The flush of guilt engendered by this unkind thought about one sister was swiftly displaced by her consideration of the other. Dear, sweet Olivia, the oldest sister who had two great loves, namely books and playing their prized square pianoforte from John Broadwood & Sons, no less, a great luxury provided by their doting father. Quiet, shy and sensible Olivia, for whom the occasional and unavoidable forays into society with its balls and festive gatherings were not just a part of life to be enjoyed, but rather an exquisite form of torture to be endured. While Kitty and Alice were both aware that their continuing unmarried status was an ever–present concern for her parents, they knew that it was Olivia for whom this anxiety became more acute with every passing year. Sadly she was immune to her mother's urgings and was adamant in showing little interest in the opposite sex. And that disinterest, however gently articulated and masked by charmingly modest politesse, soon communicated itself to potential suitors and sent them in search of young ladies more amenable and approachable as prospective partners.

The ladies set off upstairs to change for dinner and Sir Joshua settled down with his beloved Times, all the excitement of James' arrival having caused him to fall distressingly behind in his usual reading schedule, a matter he generally made every effort to complete before the dinner gong sounded.

When it did so a little later he laid aside his paper with a sigh and a lingering glance of regret at a tantalisingly unread section upon the last page. He met his wife and daughters in the entrance hall as they descended the stairs and absently noted that they were all somewhat more elaborately dressed than a family dinner would normally warrant.

Sir Joshua held out his arm and once Lady Cecilia was firmly attached to it, the pair led their brood into the dining room.

They were in the process of seating themselves when James appeared, having apparently made a futile effort to tame his unruly hair, whereupon Sir Joshua indicated the seat beside him and they all settled into their allotted places. Jackson supervised the laying out of various courses before the assemblage, and Tom and the maid Lucy acquitted themselves very well in their tasks as servers. Conversation flowed most agreeably around the topics of the time, from the poems and travels of Lord Byron to the threat to all Europe from Napoleon and the sad state of Spain and the Spanish people's suffering under the occupation by Bonaparte.

In her usual forthright manner Kitty questioned James about his life in India. Having just finished a sizeable portion of very fine roast beef, he sipped appreciatively from his glass of claret before replying.

'Firstly may I say what a pleasure it is to dine with all of you, whom I believe I may call my family,' he said with a patent sincerity that made them all warm to him.

'I was no more than two years old when Father took me to India, which as you know is where I have spent all my life since, until very recently. That life in that faraway place is virtually all I know, but we British do tend to live and socialise together in our own cantonments or districts, and of course most are in the East India Company's armies or administration. So in some ways our social life did probably not differ greatly from that in the mother country, albeit the servants all had dark complexions and the food, even the most English of dishes, when replicated by an Indian cook somehow acquired an exotic element.'

'Father became an agent, and because he soon gained a reputation for honesty and fair dealing both with Europeans and natives, his business prospered.'

He paused with a faraway look in his eye.

'In the early days I attended the nearby garrison school, but father was dissatisfied with their efforts and from the age of ten or so engaged a tutor, a well-educated Indian lady named Mrs Khambata, a widow. She was a Parsee – an enterprising people small in number but with considerable influence, originally from Persia, followers of the ancient Zoroastrian religion and very distinct from the larger Hindoo population. I am eternally grateful to her and believe the education she gave me was infinitely superior to any other I might have received, given the place and circumstances.'

He paused and his gaze was clearly upon some place in his memory and far away from the here and now. As the pause lengthened Sir Joshua coughed politely and the sound appeared to recall him from wherever his mind had taken him.

'Father took me into the business when I was fifteen,' he continued, 'and to both our surprises I appeared to have an aptitude for it so it was not long before we were running it as partners. I suppose it was a happy life in many ways for the next dozen years or so, until the cholera took him. But that was then and now I am here and could not be happier than to be reunited with and receive such affection from my family.'

They were all much affected by his candour and straightforward manner and the rest of the evening passed extremely pleasantly. Later that night as Kitty lay in her bed with a smile, her mind was filled with pleasant thoughts of Cousin James and of colourful and fanciful imaginings of his romantic upbringing in the East, so different and remote from their own quiet life in the county, enlivened as it was merely by occasional forays to Bath and London. And just before she eventually slipped into Morpheus' embrace, the image of Olivia in a wedding dress appeared to her, looking radiantly happy, and she went to sleep unaware that her smile had metamorphosed into an unhappy frown.

# II

KITTY WAS AN habitual early riser and as was her usual practice when the day promised to be fair, had dressed and gone for a stroll in the grounds before breakfast. She was particularly fond of the large walled rose garden, her mother's pride and joy, and walked through the trees bordering the driveway as always taking quiet pleasure in her immersion in the soothing green–tinted world and accompanying birdsong that permeated the surrounding light forest with cascades of liquid notes. She crossed a patch of wildflower meadow and made her way to a weathered oaken door set in a high wall of equally weathered mossy red brick that enclosed the rose garden.

The door was ajar and she stopped abruptly and withdrew slightly as she saw cousin James sitting on a wrought iron bench in a brown study, his chin propped on his hands with that same absent and faraway look he had briefly exhibited at dinner. She stood in the doorway and observed him for some time but when there was no alteration in his posture found herself walking towards him, taking care to tread softly although she was unsure of her reason for doing so. She was virtually next to him before he became aware of her presence and leapt to his feet in some confusion.

'Kitty! Forgive me, I was deep in thought and was oblivious to your approach, I hope I did not startle you by my reaction!'

She smiled and sat down, at which he resumed his seat beside her.

'Why James, it is I who should apologise for startling you! I did not realise how deeply engrossed you were in whatever thoughts occupied you. Forgive me in turn, but is all well with you? You look somewhat pale.'

His bronzed complexion had a pallor beneath it that dissipated and returned him to his normal appearance as she spoke. He appeared to turn over her words in his mind as if trying to formulate a response before giving a embarrassed laugh.

'I am sorry, my dear Cousin, I must seem very peculiar to you! Please do not concern yourself, I assure you that I am in the best of health.'

'Well if nothing ails you, what then is it that causes you to lapse into such a profound reverie, James? It must be something of importance to you?'

He regarded her with a quixotic expression that appeared composed of equal parts of amusement, exasperation and frustration.

'Kitty, Kitty! You are not like any young woman I have ever encountered. You really do speak your mind with very little concern for propriety and social norms, do you not!'

She began to apologise for offending him but he

held up a commanding hand to stop her.

'Did I say I was offended? I do not believe so! Please do not think I spoke in protest, I beg you! It is just … rather uncommon and takes a little getting used to.' He paused and appeared to be searching for words.

'I once sustained a serious injury, of which you will probably have noticed my lasting souvenir, the oddly shaped scar on my temple. I was unconscious for days and was subsequently left with a period of time of which I have no recollection whatsoever, an opaque section of my life that resists my every attempt to exert my memory. There. You are the only person in the entire world since my dear Father to whom I have made this strange malady known.'

Kitty was utterly nonplussed by his revelation and for once in her life was in the unusual position of being entirely bereft of words.

'I should not have burdened you with my curious problem, Kitty. It was quite wrong of me. I hope to see you at breakfast,' he said, smiled wearily and patted her arm as he got to his feet and walked off towards the house. *I must think about this*, she admonished herself sternly, *and not jump to any conclusions. But I have never heard of anyone confessing to such a strange and peculiarly specific malady.* But her curiosity was now at fever pitch, wondering what could possibly have caused such an extraordinary blanking out of memory, and her character was such that she simply could not abide not knowing something when she felt certain there were unknown things, and possibly very interesting things, to be found and be transported from the darkness of the unknown to the light of the known.

It happened that all the family arrived in the breakfast room within moments of each other and after the initial pleasantries the conversation became sporadic as the sound of cutlery on china and toast, rolls, butter and preserves being consumed and cups tinkling on saucers quietly pervaded the room. In a show of familial affection that amazed his wife and daughters Sir Joshua generously and unprecedentedly divided and shared his copy of the Times with James, into which uncle and step–nephew happily immersed themselves as they sipped their tea.

'It promises to be an exceptionally fine day and I would very much like to go riding, Papa,' said Kitty when breakfast was done, 'will you ride with me?'

There were stables at Longton Manor, although they only had two mounts apart from the carriage horses. Her mother and sisters not only had no interest whatsoever in riding but actively tried to discourage Kitty from a pursuit all three of them deemed unnecessary, unladylike and terrifyingly hazardous. As neither of her parents would countenance her riding alone, doting, compliant and persuadable though they might be in many other matters, Kitty was consequently dependant upon Sir Joshua accompanying her, which he was seldom willing to do without a specific destination such as visiting a neighbour or having some business in Wallstock, their nearest town. On those occasions when her longing to ride became overwhelming she would order Tom, the lad who doubled as stable boy and Ned the gardener's assistant as well as an occasional footman to accompany her, but his awestruck demeanour, his unusually protuberant Adam's apple and inability to articulate a coherent sentence greatly detracted from her enjoyment.

'I think not, my dear,' replied Sir Joshua. 'I have some correspondence to attend to, and I have yet to complete the first page of the Times. I say, James, would you care to accompany Kitty? I believe I can say without hyperbole or any exaggeration caused by parental affection that she is a first–rate rider, and you would be doing her a great favour as it is one of her passions!'

'How could I possibly refuse,' said James with a smile. 'It would be my very great pleasure to accompany you. Shall we meet at the stables in say, half an hour? Splendid!'

Sir Joshua instructed Jackson to have Tom prepare the horses and repaired to the drawing room to re–immerse himself in the Times with a contented sigh, the excuse of correspondence having been relegated as of lesser import and quickly forgotten. Kitty changed into her russet riding habit and matching bonnet and made her way to the stables where Tom was waiting patiently with her mare Bella by the mounting block. She ascended the steps and settled herself securely in the side saddle with the ease of long experience when James arrived, cutting a dashing figure, or so Kitty thought, wearing a fashionable green frock coat, white and green striped waistcoat and jaunty yellow gloves. Tom led out her father's horse, an impressive grey called Balthazar, whose imposing name and appearance belied a sweet and biddable nature, qualities in which her own mount Bella was somewhat deficient, requiring a strong hand to control her occasional wilfulness.

'This is your home, dear Cousin, so I would be honoured if you would show me some of your favourite places to ride,' said James and Kitty smiled and nodded, gently tapped Bella's haunch with her riding crop and they set of at a brisk walk. James forged slightly ahead as he sped up to a trot down the drive and Kitty observed him with a frown. Her liking for his attractive person and open and pleasant manner had considerable weight on the scales of her opinion. But these were known, quantifiable and straightforward elements to consider, while on the other side of the scales was her instinct from the very start that he was holding something back, confirmed by his admission of a most strange memory problem that, until she knew precisely what it signified, counterbalanced and outweighed the positive. And even weightier than any concerns of her own was that she could see Mama had set her heart on marrying off Olivia to James, and her love for her quiet, unassuming older sister and knowledge of her parent's anxieties in that regard added a further, decisive weight. In truth it was only her own quickening interest that she could set against all these troubling elements, an interest she was unwilling to admit to herself.

He turned in his saddle and smiled, slowing Balthazar until she was alongside him.

'You must forgive me for drawing ahead so rudely, but it is all still so new to me and I was quite distracted! After a lifetime in the tropics the sights of the English countryside are still as strange and exotic to me as the jungles of the Sunderban would be to you. Oh, of course, how foolish of me, there is no reason at all why you should be familiar with the name. It is a mangrove forest on the edge of the Bay of Bengal, not too far from Calcutta, a singular and otherworldly place where the trees grow not just to the coast but even out into the sea and it is abundant with wildlife including many dangerous tigers, for which it is famous, or should I rather say, infamous. It could not be more different than this tranquil and orderly vista before me. Where that place is, at least in part, nature wild, savage and primordially bloody, here I am surrounded by nature tamed, ordered and redesigned for our wellbeing both spiritual and physical.'

He looked embarrassed and laughed self–deprecatingly as he apologised for getting somewhat carried away. Their conversation flowed easily after that and Kitty found herself telling him all sorts of little anecdotes and pointing out things that were of interest to her. That was where she had first jumped a fence, there was the meadow across which she had galloped and fallen off her horse, happily escaping with a few bruises, and had sworn Tom to secrecy and kept her fall from her parents.

'And yet you have entrusted me with your secrets, Cousin.' he said with a bow from his saddle. 'I am honoured by your confidence and you may be sure that my lips are sealed! Please do show me more of the places that are special to you.'

They rode on up a large meadow to the top of a rise and reined in their mounts to partake of a particularly fine view over forests, fields, distant villages and on and on to the hazy blue horizon and infinity. She was about to confide that this was one of her favourite places because of the view when he pointed to a very substantial property on the flat ground beyond the hill upon which they stood, surrounded by extensive manicured formal grounds in the French style.

'And what, pray tell is that? It seems very grand!'

'That is Wraxton Place, the family seat of Hugo Crasmere, the current Earl of Wallstock. They are fearful snobs and as Papa is a mere Baronet and therefore not deemed to be of the peerage they consider us to be most inferior. We only socialise once or twice a year when they hold a ball of sufficient numbers to cast the net wider and include small fry such as the local doctor and vicar and ourselves, so I hardly know them at all.'

She dismissed the Crasmeres with an airy flick of the hand while James sat still as a statue before turning to her with a smile that was palpably strained.

'Crasmere, you say? How is it that I know the name? It is familiar and yet I am not aware of any such acquaintance … how curious.'

'I may have an answer for you, James! As I recall a few years ago there was some sort of scandal – I am afraid the details escape me, as it was of no particular interest to me at the time. I do recollect that it involved two of the Crasmere boys and both Hugo, who at that time was actually then the younger son and his older brother Charles were sent off to tour India under the care of an uncle there! Perhaps you knew them?'

James shook his head.

'No, I do not believe so. Perhaps my father may have mentioned them, that is probably it. It would not have been surprising in the least if I had never met them, for India is after all an immense country, sufficiently so to be classed as a sub–continent. And if memory serves I believe there are over one hundred thousand of us British there. And of course to many of the English who came out as officers, directors and administrators we Stricklands were very much trade, and for much of the time would not have moved in the same circles unless we were required to make up the numbers for some function or other.'

'Well, there was some kind of family tragedy while they were out there in India,' continued Kitty. 'I don't know the details, but whatever happened, I am afraid the elder son Charles met with some kind of fatal accident there, I do not know of what nature, but in any case he died which is why the title then went to Hugo.'

'Ah, I see,' he said, and Kitty noticed that his tanned knuckles were white as if he were squeezing the reins with all his might. They turned around and rode back to Longton Manor, and in stark contrast to their loquacious outward excursion, James had relapsed into his reverie and was distant and hardly uttered a word all the way.

# III

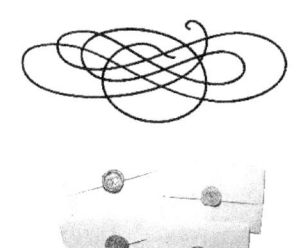

WHEN KITTY RETURNED from riding with James she went upstairs and changed from her riding habit into her favourite day dress for the summer, light, white, sleeveless with pretty lace trim and one of her most comfortable garments. With a last glance in the mirror she proceeded downstairs to the drawing room where she found her mother seated next to her father, radiating barely suppressed excitement.

'Ah, Kitty, capital! I have a matter of *great* import to discuss with your father and you should be present. Your sisters have taken the phaeton to Wallstock to inspect the latest fashions at Whittaker's Emporium, so it is just the three of us. Quickly now, before James appears.'

Sir Joshua had been paying her little attention, determinedly entrenched behind the bulwark of his newspaper and Lady Cecilia impatiently tapped his arm with her fan, her usual tactic to attract his attention on those occasions when he appeared determinedly recalcitrant to provide it to her. Though clearly tearing himself from his beloved Times with great reluctance he nonetheless completed the difficult transition from the affairs of the world to his drawing room and smiled fondly at her, which he knew from experience would disarm her and dissipate her impatience.

'Yes, my love, what is it?'

'We must give a ball!' she exclaimed with great force. 'It is at *least* two years since the last time and that was but a small affair, hardly worthy of being called a ball at all! If we are to have any chance whatsoever of bringing poor Olivia's lamentable spinsterhood to an end and advancing her into James' affections, the time is now, before his condition of desirable availability becomes common knowledge! For once that happens, the local harridans will lose no time in mustering their legions of unmarried daughters and begin their determined assault! What do you say, Sir?'

Many things went through Sir Joshua's mind before he replied, the uppermost of these being the great expense of the proposed enterprise. Their situation was comfortable, it was true. His grandfather had been formidably adept at trading and investing, with an unerring nose for correctly assessing who would do what and when to buy low and when to sell high accordingly. His investments had more than secured the family's financial future, especially as he had, in addition to his legacy, expended considerable sums upon repairs and decoration and upgrading Longton Manor, thereby ensuring the long–term solidity and integrity of its fabric.

Sir Joshua looked up the portrait of him by the famous painter Thomas Lawrence, not long after he had painted his first royal commission, a portrait of Queen Charlotte. It had been completed soon before Grandpapa's death, and Sir Joshua always felt guilty for thinking that he looked not only prosperous but somewhat self satisfied, which, in all fairness, he had had every right to be.

Despite the fact that he shared his oldest daughter's preference for a quiet and ordered life, he understood perfectly well that her future must be secured, accompanied by a background uneasiness that he had perhaps been somewhat dilatory in assisting his wife in furthering that goal. Thus it was that he patted Lady Cecilia's arm with unfeigned acquiescence.

'What do I say, Madam? What I say is, of *course* we must, my dear, you are quite right. I must needs leave the details to you and Mrs Thrupp as you know I should be of little use in such matters.'

His wife beamed, leaned over and kissed his whiskers before hurrying off to consult the housekeeper and begin the Herculean task that now lay before her. Sir Joshua marked the strange expression on Kitty's face and took her hand.

'Are you all right, sweet child? You do not seem excited by the prospect of a ball, even though I know you have enjoyed other such occasions. Is there anything you wish to tell me?'

Kitty looked at her father's loving and guileless visage and horrifyingly imagined retorting with her true feelings. *I want him for myself! But Mama is right, we must see to Olivia above all else and I will swallow my true feelings and encourage him in her direction. I will. I really will.*

At that moment James entered the drawing room and hesitated, sensing the intimate moment between father and daughter.

'Forgive me, I did not mean to intrude!' He made to leave but Sir Joshua relinquished his daughter's hand and waved him over.

'Nonsense, dear boy, how many times must I tell you this is now your home and therefore you cannot and do not intrude in the slightest! Come and sit, we have some news! There is to be a ball here at Longton Manor! And you shall be our guest of honour, how's that, eh?'

'How delightful, and of course I am honoured! Uncle, I know it's a bit of a cheek, but is there any possibility including the Crasmeres of Wraxton Place? We saw their grand house in the distance on our ride this morning. There is the slimmest of chances I may have met the brothers in India and would like to see if the surviving brother recalls me, or I him.'

'A tragedy, that, a double tragedy what with the scandal and then the heir's death. But of course, my boy, I shall speak to my lady wife about it although I strongly suspect it was her intention in any case. I should caution you, however, that *inviting* them is one thing, and whether or not they *accept* the invitation is quite another. I tend not to notice these matters, but I have heard that they can be deucedly stand–offish.'

Lady Cecilia now existed in an unapproachable ferment of pleasurable anxiety and preparation, and constantly sought out Mrs Thrupp whenever a new thought on some aspect of the ball occurred to her. A lesser mortal might have buckled under the constant onslaught and been tempted to lose their temper or hand in their notice, but the housekeeper was made of sterner stuff. Her mistress' words washed over her like ocean waves shattering on an immovable rocky shore and eventually the lady of the house would run out of words and ideas, at which point Mrs Thrupp would nod understandingly and utter her usual response on such occasions.

'Absolutely, my Lady, just leave it to me.' Whereupon Mrs Thrupp would do precisely what she thought was for the best, secure in the knowledge that Lady Cecilia would assume that whatever was done had been what she had requested, as, with all due modesty, the housekeeper inevitably did know what was for the best.

Kitty determined to make a particular effort to put her own feelings to one side and to commence a campaign upon Olivia's behalf. After much thought she settled upon a two–pronged attack; on the one hand to compel herself to place distance between herself and James so that he would look elsewhere for female company and attachment, and by the same token do all she could to nudge him and her sister towards each other by whatever stratagems presented themselves.

The next day proved as fine as the day before, and Lady Cecilia rushed off in the phaeton after breakfast to commence attacking her seemingly endless list of preparations and decisions for the ball, eagerly accompanied by Alice for whom the myriad tasks to be accomplished were very much an endeavour of high interest and excitement. The printers were to be visited and consulted on the choice of designs for the invitations, menus and dance cards, as was the florist to settle upon the quantity, styles and colour schemes of the arrangements, all to be approved before finalisation by Mrs Thrupp. A round of visits to ladies of her acquaintance in the vicinity had to be made in order to beg and borrow additional kitchen staff, serving staff and footmen. Lady Cecilia and the other ladies were members of an informal cabal who, while respected and prominent in local society, were not too exalted to understand the need for mutual assistance and the concomitant mutual minimising of expense for larger events.

Engaging musicians and settling upon a musical programme was facilitated by consultation with the seemingly ubiquitous services and wide–ranging contacts of Augustus Whittaker, rotund and bewhiskered proprietor of Whittaker's Emporium. There were lengthy discussions with cook and the housekeeper, agonising over the menu with one eye upon the cost and the other upon the necessity of not appearing in any way mean or sparing.

His wife tested Sir Joshua's good nature to the limit by constantly fretting and checking with him to ensure that all the necessary quantities of champagnes and wines were delivered in good time and that there would not be the slightest chance of running out of these essential social lubricants. And of course new dresses were required for all the Strickland ladies to whom Whittaker's Emporium soon became something of a second home as catalogues were pored over, seamstresses consulted, materials fingered consideringly, colours judged not only upon their own merits but also to ensure the avoidance of any clashes when the Strickland ladies made their entrance together.

Upon Lady Cecilia fell the particular duty of instructing her husband as to precisely what was required for his and James' outfits to ensure their wardrobes were up to the occasion, but also that Sir

Joshua would rigorously inspect the servant's liveries for the avoidance of any horrors such as stains, wear and tear and frayed cuffs.

Time passed and the invitations were duly printed and delivered and the Strickland household waited with bated breath for the responses to arrive. Even Kitty and Olivia could not help succumbing – although to a considerably lesser degree – to the pre–ball excitement verging on mania and hysteria that gripped the household at Longton Manor.

Whenever a rider or liveried footman was heard crunching across the gravel driveway Lady Cecilia would take her life in her hands and fly down the stairs or out of the drawing room at a pace that would have seemed well–nigh impossible under normal circumstances. But it would have been perfectly clear to even the most casual observer that these circumstances were anything but normal. The drawing room became the battle headquarters of Lady Cecilia, combining the roles of General, tactician and Quartermaster in consultation with Mrs Thrupp as lists were reviewed and revised and tradesmen and staff instructed. The relative importance of the particular guest when their reply to their invitation arrived was easily ascertainable by the pitch and volume of Lady Cecilia's exclamations upon opening the envelopes, be they high notes of satisfaction or baser notes of disappointment. Happily for both her and consequently the household there were mercifully few of the latter, and of those non–attending guests Sir Joshua commented laconically that their absence might well be better appreciated than their presence.

On the second day the trickle of responses became a flood and Lady Cecilia worked furiously at her desk, prising open wax seals and crossing out and adding ticks to her lists and keeping a nail–biting running total of acceptances. Wearily picking up yet another missive she froze as she saw the expensively gold–embossed coat of arms on the equally expensive thick folded paper. It depicted a golden leopard rampant on a field of azure surmounted by a decorative helm with streamers. Being an avid student of the heraldry of all those aristocratic families with whom there was even the remotest chance of contact she instantly recognised it as being that of the Earl of Wallstock.

Her breath came in shallow gasps as she carefully worked the wax seal off the paper taking great care to do as little damage as possible and unfolded the single sheet of … 'parchment!' she whispered in awe, feeling it's weight and stiffness and admiring the crest repeated at the top of the letter.

*My Dear Lady Cecilia*

*We are in receipt of your kind invitation to a ball at Longton Manor, for which consideration we wish to express our gratitude.*

*As I understand it, Sir Joshua's nephew Mr James Strickland is thereby to be introduced to local society and we are pleased to assist in smoothing his path after so many years in the Orient. We therefore graciously accept.*

*On a personal note I am well aware of how essential it is to have a firm grip upon the numbers on such occasions as the slightest deviations may distressingly unbalance even the most carefully laid of plans. So as one Lady to another please be advised that my son the Earl and I will be accompanied by my youngest son Frederick and their sister Emilia.*

*Georgiana*
*Dowager Countess of Wallstock*

Lady Cecilia's triumphant cries resounded throughout Longton Manor as she summoned her family, feeling as if she were about to burst and unable to wait even a second longer than absolutely necessary to impart the news. Sir Joshua's broadsheet dropped to the floor in crumpled disorder as he stared with astonishment at his wife who seemed to be in the grip of some manner of paroxysm as she leapt to her feet and began beating his arm with her fan in a most agitated not to say rather painful manner.

'Whatever is the matter, my love?' he enquired with some concern as he surreptitiously rubbed his arm, but she shook her head emphatically.

'They must all be here! Where *are* those girls! Ah, at last!'

Her three daughters ran rather than walked into the drawing room and halted abruptly at the sight of their wild–eyed mother hitting their father with her fan and grinning maniacally.

'Sir Joshua! My lovely darling girls! *They are coming! They have accepted*! She even addressed me as *one Lady to another!* I can scarcely believe it! I am overcome!'

She brandished the letter with the air of a victor in battle displaying colours heroically captured from the enemy.

'Husband! Here! Read it out aloud so that I may be satisfied this is not some hallucinatory phantom but wonderful reality!'

Sir Joshua took the proffered letter and read it aloud carefully and precisely while his wife lay back blissfully on a sofa with her eyes closed, repeating phrases under her breath as he read them.

*My dear Lady Cecilia …*

*We feel bound to smooth his path …*
*On a personal note …*
*As one Lady to another …*
*… their youngest son Frederick and his sister Emilia …*

There was a moment's silence when Sir Joshua had finished reading the letter before Lady Cecilia's eyes flew open and her gratified smile evaporated, metamorphosing into one of sudden alarm.

'My dears! Do you know what this means! Not for one moment did I expect the highest–ranking family in the county to accept our invitation and laid our plans accordingly. But now, in light of this joyous news, all our arrangements have become *utterly* inadequate *at a stroke* and we must check every detail and change whatever we can in the time remaining! Just think of it! The Earl and all his family here, in Longton Manor as our guests! Oh dear oh dear oh dear, however shall we manage it! But manage it we must! Girls! Let us seek out Mrs Thrupp and the kitchen staff! She and I shall require your assistance else we shall fall at the hurdle and become a laughingstock!'

The four women hurried out of the room chattering excitedly, leaving Sir Joshua alone to retrieve his battered Times from the floor with a resigned sigh. His wife might have won a great victory, but his newspaper would never be quite the same. And the thought of the augmented expense of putting on a show fit for the Earl and his family did not improve his mood in the slightest. His eyes fell upon the Coat of Arms embossed on the letter and he took the time to read the Crasmere's motto.

*'Audaces Fatum Adiuvat,'* he said under his breath, 'Fate Favours The Bold.'

'And the rich,' he added as an afterthought.

# IV

THE DAYS PASSED and the myriad plans and arrangements for the ball inched forward with endless adjustments and revisions and family debates agonising over the details and especially which of the upper ranks of the local aristocracy who had not yet replied might attend and further enhance the occasion, thus raising the tone and not disappointing the Crasmeres. It was unfortunate that Alice's boundless enthusiasm and love of balls was sadly not matched by any vestige of organisational ability and it fell to Kitty and Olivia to assist their mother with the inevitable problems and crises that arose and subsided with the regularity of waves upon a shore, and usually resulted in them jointly handing the problem over to the housekeeper.

'Would you care to ride with me again?' James asked Kitty on the evening following the news of their exalted guests, and seemed quite put out when she said that unfortunately her mother had great need of her, particularly now that all the arrangements for the ball had to be revisited and improved wherever possible.

'I am sorry to hear you say that,' he said. 'I very much enjoyed our ride the other day and was hoping to hear more about your adventures and charming favourite places.'

He looked so disappointed that she almost weakened, but reminded herself of her solemn resolve and spoke words that belied her true feelings, suppressed with some difficulty.

'I too am sorry, James, but there is simply nothing to be done about it. I know! While I feel certain that tomorrow Mama will keep me fully occupied for all of the day, I do believe that for the morning at least, Olivia is not required. I know she does not ride, but it would be a great kindness were you to take her on a walk, should the weather hold. I do feel I have somewhat monopolised you since your arrival and would take it as a favour to me if you were to get to know her better. She is wonderfully accomplished and well read, you know, far more so than I, and I am sure she could keep you better entertained than I ever could!'

The sadness she saw in his eyes wrenched at her heart and almost made her abandon her campaign on Olivia's behalf at the first hurdle, but she steeled herself and smiled a dissembling smile that she hoped indicated nothing more than the desire for her sister to have a pleasant walk.

'Are you certain you cannot … ' he began and she forced herself to laugh.

'*Quite* certain, Cousin! May I inform Olivia of your outing tomorrow?'

He hesitated for a long moment before nodding,

smiling perfunctorily and turning away. Every fibre of her being wanted to hurry after him and say *No, no! It is* I *who wants you!* but she was both stubborn and determined once she had embarked upon a course of action, and held her tongue.

She knocked on Olivia's door and closed it behind her. Her sister was at her dressing table, brushing her hair now freed from it's usual confines of ribbons and combs. It was dark and similar in tone to Kitty's but somehow more subdued than her younger sister's exuberant locks.

'Why Kitty, what is it? Is something the matter?'

'No, no my darling sister! I have some news that will be of interest to you. I have just been speaking with our cousin James and he intimated that he would take pleasure in accompanying you for a walk after breakfast tomorrow! What do you think of that!'

Olivia sat very still for quite some time before speaking with a puzzled look on her face.

'Truly? Is that not somewhat strange? He and I have exchanged little more than a few words since he arrived, and those have mostly been mere pleasantries. I was rather under the impression that it was *you* and not I who held most interest for him!'

Kitty forced herself to laugh in a manner that she hoped suggested light–hearted self–deprecation.

'Oh Olivia! You are so innocent of the ways of the world! Yes, I practically forced him to ride with me when Papa would not, and we passed the time pleasantly enough, but he did enquire after you on several occasions.'

Olivia's pale cheeks turned a delicate shade of pink, just discernible in the flickering candlelight of her bedroom and Kitty had to exert herself to will away her qualms at lying to her sister for probably the first time in their lives. She had not anticipated how painful it would be, nor how strong her consequent feelings of guilt.

'Well if you are *certain* that is what he said, I am sure it would be a pleasant enough way to pass the morning, so you may tell him I am agreeable.'

But then her face clouded over and she held up a hand.

'No, no, wait! I cannot do it! Mama will almost certainly need me, there is so much still to be done!'

'Hush, I will do whatever is necessary and in any case it will only be for an hour or two, and the world will surely not come to an end as a consequence! Let us sleep now so that we may begin tomorrow eager and refreshed!'

The sisters embraced and Kitty left Olivia examining herself in the mirror, her expression saying as clearly as if she had spoken, *why would he want to walk with me?*

In the event Lady Cecilia rushed off with Alice after breakfast, and Kitty made herself scarce in the sewing room, the one with the window seat from which she had first spied James. She watched Olivia walk down the drive with him and noted with a simultaneous sense of approval and a pang of jealousy that her sister had chosen one of her best summer dresses and bonnet and was absent–mindedly twirling a dainty parasol that served both to ward off the sun and to keep James at arm's length. She watched until they had exited the gates and disappeared from view and tried to imagine their conversation, but when she realised what she was doing and that it was accompanied by an unladylike frown, she shook herself and went downstairs to see if there was anything she could do in Lady Cecilia's absence.

She found herself in the library, idly in search of a book to read that would be more interesting than her last and utterly unmemorable choice. She settled upon a recent acquisition from Hillman's, a bookshop in Wallstock and a favourite haunt of hers. It was an anonymous publication called *Zastrozzi* that bore only the initials P.B.S., newly published, and when the avuncular proprietor saw her pick it up while browsing he informed her *sotto voce* and with a conspiratorial wink that the author was in fact Percy Bysshe Shelley, and that a critic had branded it's main character as "… one of the most savage and improbable demons that ever issued from a diseased brain." And Kitty being Kitty, after that it was quite unthinkable to her that she should not purchase it and decide for herself.

No sooner had she perused the first few pages than Olivia came into the room and drifted around aimlessly, trailing her fingers absently along shelves and tracing the titles of books with her fingertips.

'What are you doing, Olivia?' she asked and was rewarded with a smile whose happiness both filled and gripped her heart painfully in the same instant.

'Dear Kitty, I am beginning to think that you were right, I *do* believe he may be developing certain feelings towards me! How extraordinary that I had no inkling of it before! But there is a reserve to him, do you not find it so? He is polite, obliging, and can be amusing when he wishes, but … oh Kitty, how can I describe it? It is thus far and no further with him, as if there is some impenetrable boundary beyond which one may not pass. Am I being foolish? Have you nothing to say?'

'Of *course* I am happy for you, my dearest sister, how could I not be? As to his occasional reticence … we do not *really* know what his life in India and indeed life in India in general was like, and it may simply be that there are times when he feels like a fish out of water now that he is back in England. I am sure it must be some such thing. Do not concern yourself, Olivia. The longer he is here the more he will become accustomed to our ways and feel free to speak his mind, depend upon it.'

Olivia threw her arms around her sister and kissed her on the cheek.

'Thank you Kitty! You are always the sensible one who sees how things really are and knows what needs to be done. I don't know what any of us would do without you!'

They saw little of James over the next few days as he occupied himself with the business of finding a home through the good offices of Messrs Finch & Appleby, the foremost surveyors, auctioneers and land agents in the county with premises in Wallstock, and had faithfully promised the Stricklands one and all to inform them the very instant he had a possible residence in his sights. It proved, however, to be easier said than done. The county was something of a rural backwater and most properties of the type he sought were owned by families who had been annoyingly immovable for generations, and the helpful junior partner and surveyor Mr Ernest Bagstock who had been assigned to assist him would throw up his hands despairingly by way of an apology for the current dearth of suitable properties.

On one occasion Kitty was standing on the High

Street pavement in Wallstock enjoying the warm breeze and blue skies of another fine day, while her mother concluded some interminable negotiation at Whittaker's Emporium. She happened to spy James emerging from the house she knew was the surgery and home of Dr David Astley, a distant relative of some noble family and a society physician of some renown who had forsaken the bright lights of London and chosen to spend his semi–retirement in his substantial property in Wallstock, nonetheless keeping his hand in, as it were, by restricting his patient list to the foremost families in the county, not least because they were the only ones able to afford the not inconsiderable fees he commanded. Kitty watched as the two men shook hands and the doctor patted James reassuringly on the arm before his visitor hurried away, his face creased in a frown. She debated with herself whether to pursue him and to enquire after his health, but on balance felt her compulsive need to *know* and her insatiable curiosity had somehow tainted her genuine concern for him, so in the end she held her tongue in the hope that he would confide in her, which in the event he sadly did not.

'Only a week to go!' exclaimed Lady Cecilia one morning after breakfast, fanning herself furiously as the day was one of the warmest so far that summer. The days of frenetic activity were now behind them until the day itself arrived, and it finally seemed that all matters had been settled and all the necessary preparations arranged. And in the background was the soothing knowledge that the redoubtable Mrs Thrupp's eagle eye could be relied upon to tackle any deficiencies. At that moment cousin James entered the room with an excited smile, brandishing a letter.

'My dear family, as you know I have been seeking a home with the assistance of Messrs Finch & Appleby, and have just received a note from them, from Earnest Bagstock, their head surveyor, a most excellent sort of fellow other than suffering from an over–fondness of underlining words for emphasis in his correspondence – who has been most helpful to me. Do you by any chance know a property called Lionhurst in the vicinity?'

'Why yes,' replied Sir Joshua, 'it is no more than an hour or so by carriage from here. As to the owner himself, I must confess that I only knew him very slightly as he was an Army man through and through, and had little interest in his home or society or county matters, and has in any case been away fighting in the wars for some time now. In fact I have heard it said that Major Harris – for if I recall correctly that is his name – sold off a goodly part of the estate's land both in order to settle his father's debts and to finance his military career. He was not a sociable man, by all accounts, and kept himself very much to himself. Why do you ask?'

'This note informs me that word has just reached Finch & Appleby – who manage his estate in his absence – that Major Harris was killed in Portugal no more than three days ago,' replied James. 'Allow me to read the letter to you in its entirety.'

*'My dear Mr Strickland,*
*I beg to inform you that we have but a few moments ago received news that the owner of a local property known as Lionhurst, a Major Harris who served in Wellington's army in Crauford's Light Brigade, was killed in a vast explosion at the Castle Fortress of Almeida along with I*

*believe up to six hundred of our men. As I understand it, a French shell ignited the fortress' magazine, hence the shocking number of casualties.*

*Doleful and sombre though this news may be, I would be remiss in my professional duty to you were I not to point out that our firm (and now yourself) are at this particular moment <u>the sole possessors of this news</u>, and however lamentable and even unseemly it may appear to even suggest it, we are nonetheless <u>briefly</u> in a <u>uniquely advantageous</u> position. It is an <u>unrivalled opportunity</u> for you to acquire the property without the often costly inconvenience of rival buyers.*

*As I believe the property is admirably suited to the requirements you have been kind enough to describe to me in some detail, kindly therefore permit me to be so bold as to suggest <u>most urgently</u> that you and I visit the property <u>at your very earliest convenience</u>?*

*I remain, Sir, your obedient servant,*
*Ernest Bagstock, LLB.'*

'What do you think?' said James, putting down the letter and scrutinising their reaction.

'Oh you must!' burst out Kitty. 'I know it may well appear unseemly to some, but the fact of the matter is that the poor man has heroically given his life for his country, and no matter how sad that may be, no purpose will be served by delaying. You must go immediately, James! Oh! May I ride with you? Poor Bella needs some exercise and it may be of use to have someone familiar with these great houses by your side!'

'Why, nothing would please me more!' exclaimed James. 'Come, let us change and meet in the stables in, say twenty minutes?'

As she made her way out of the Drawing Room Kitty caught the hurt look in Olivia's eyes and cursed her impulsiveness. However this variation from her avowed plans was soon displaced by the excitement of an unusual occasion, not only the secret pleasure of a ride with James before he became too attached to Olivia, but also the irresistible curiosity that was never far below the surface was now awakened and eager to see Lionhurst of which she had only heard vaguely that it was a well–kept and imposing property. And of course, that one day might come to be James' home. And Olivia's, she mentally added with some reluctance.

# V

THEY RODE AT a goodly pace to the offices of Messrs Finch & Appleby and once there it was a matter of minutes for the tall figure of Mr Bagstock to emerge and, having taken great care to position a fashionable beaver top hat just so at a rakish angle upon his unruly ginger hair, to drape himself with surprisingly sprightly agility and expertise onto a good–looking bay roan. After being introduced to Kitty the three of them were soon cantering down the Oxford Road which eventually passed close by to Lionhurst.

'We have arrived, so if you would be so good as to follow me?' said Mr Bagstock, and led them off the main country road through a narrow lane that cut through a belt of dappled woodland and when they emerged after a few hundred yards they found themselves at an open gate that had seen better days, the eroded and weather–beaten stone gateposts surmounted by two aloof figures barely recognisable as the seated lions they represented. But it was not the gateposts that made them rein in their mounts. The path before them led across a vast meadow densely crowded with a riot of wildflower colours, beyond which stood Lionhurst itself.

It could not have been more pleasing a sight if the painter Constable himself had set one of his masterpieces before them. High white clouds obscured some of the hitherto blue sky, but the sun shone through a gap and bathed the house in a shaft of golden light. Slender columns supported a modest portico that floated upon them to half the height of the building and imparted a pleasing sense of airy lightness. All the detail other than the pleasantly mellow brickwork was finished in white stone, and rows of large windows the first floor gave a welcoming look to the well–proportioned wings on either side. There was little in the way of gardens other than a somewhat dispirited and haphazard floral display in the centre of the circular gravelled drive.

'Oh, *James!*' Kitty was unaware of the breathy desire in her voice. 'Oh James, it is lovely! There is so much that could be done with it! You must acquire it if you can! You *must!*'

James regarded her quizzically for a moment before turning to Mr Bagstock, who was watching them attentively

'You heard my cousin, did you not, Mr Bagstock? It seems I have my instructions, so shall we inspect the interior whilst you elucidate the steps involved in its acquisition?'

They dismounted and a sleepy footman in creased breeches and wearing nothing else but a loose shirt emerged and took charge of their horses. Bagshaw led them into a marble–floored entrance hall that extended the whole height of the edifice and was simple and classically elegant without being overdecorated or overburdened with statuary. A finely carved mahogany staircase led to the upper floors. After inspecting some of the bedrooms they returned downstairs and their guide took them into a sparsely furnished drawing room. As with some of the upper rooms, there were signs of neglect in patches of water–stained wallpaper and cracks and missing sections of plasterwork. They sat down on a sofa that sagged alarmingly beneath their weight.

'I knew at once that Lionhurst would satisfy all your requirements, Mr Strickland, and from both your reactions, if I may say so, I feel most gratified to be vindicated in that conviction. The situation regarding the disposition of the property is as follows. The late Major's only living relative is an aged aunt who inhabits a comfortable cottage just a few hundred yards beyond the gardens at the rear of the property. As part of my supervisory role here during the late Major's prolonged absences I visit her from time to time to ensure all her needs are met, and I can say with some certainty that all she wishes for what remains of her life is to live comfortably in the cottage which she has come to love and regard as her permanent home. The Major made many attempts but was quite unable to persuade her to live in the big house, as she calls it.'

He paused and regarded them consideringly before heaving a resigned sigh.

'I can see that you are a man of honour, Mr Strickland, is it not so, Miss Kitty?' He continued speaking without waiting for a reply. 'From our previous conversations I understand that what you require is not so much an estate as a home. This property is both ideal and unusual in that respect, in that most of the land has been sold off thereby greatly reducing the potential income and consequently the price, to which it is directly correlated. If I may be so bold, may I suggest an arrangement whereby the old lady's wish is fulfilled and she is guaranteed an uninterrupted enjoyment of her home until her time comes, as sadly but inevitably it must come to us all. She was entirely reliant upon the Major for all things and has virtually no income of her own. I will suggest a figure I had previously calculated and believe is fair to all parties, namely £47,000, which takes into account the limited land and concomitant reduction in revenue, the condition and size of the main building, and the rent–free occupation of the cottage for her lifetime. And of course the sale proceeds will more than comfortably see to her every conceivable needs in her few remaining years. Is all this acceptable to you?'

Kitty's heart sank upon hearing such an unimaginably enormous sum and she watched James closely for any hesitation or sign that it might be beyond his means.

'Absolutely capital, Mr Bagshaw, I am in total agreement with everything you have said, so I would be most grateful if you would proceed without delay. And if you can bring this endeavour to a successful conclusion, I assure you I will not be reticent in demonstrating my appreciation.'

They stood and James shook Mr Bagshaw warmly by the hand, which appeared to both surprise and please the surveyor immensely.

He proved to be a genial companion and let slip

that in his leisure time had aspirations to be an artist. Kitty insisted upon seeing his work and in her usual way of getting what she wanted, overcame his bashful reticence and would not take no for an answer. When they arrived she was favourably impressed by the cleanliness and neatness of his well–appointed apartments that occupied the entire upper floor above Hillman's bookshop in the High Street.

His shyness evaporated the moment he unrolled the first canvas, a delightful study of a wildflower meadow much like the one they had just traversed to get to Lionhurst, a riot of colours that were somehow true and believable and never lapsed into garishness. After looking through a selection of his work she perched on the edge of the only armchair, smoothed her dress and regarded him archly.

'Why Mr Bagstock! You undoubtedly have a talent, such a light hand that can magick the sunlight to shine from a piece of canvas. Wonderful. Upon another occasion I would like to bring the rest of my family to see your work.'

Her eyes suddenly widened and she clapped her hands and pointed a finger at the unfortunate surveyor, who stepped back wondering what offense he might have committed.

'Mama has been tearing her hair out trying to find an artist to chalk the ballroom floor, she has taken it into her head that if she does not succeed, our splendid ball will be disastrous and utterly ruined. Would you consider such a commission?'

'I have seen such decoration on a ballroom floor once or twice, but have never attempted any such thing. I am really not sure … '

'They are usually patterns and flowers and such–

like, are they not? And in the end their purpose is to enhance the decor, mask any imperfections on the floor and to give the dancers a better grip and prevent them from slipping. So none will cast too critical an eye upon your creation and sadly after the first dance it will have been all but destroyed. Oh I beg you, Mr Bagshaw, please do this kindness for us!'

It was only upon their return when they cantered through the gates of Longton Manor that Kitty became cognisant of the fact that she and James had been deep in animated conversation about Lionhurst after leaving the self–effacing Mr Bagshaw's apartment, who had proved not only to have artistic talent but also to be knowledgeable, amusing and well–educated, having read law at Cambridge before joining his father's firm. She fell abruptly silent for the short stretch remaining, occasioning puzzled glances from her companion.

Lady Cecilia was delighted that she now had an artist to decorate the dance floor, but Kitty was distracted from her mother's happiness by the hurt in Olivia's eyes which was like a dagger to her heart, and when the family retired for the night she knocked softly on her sister's door before slipping in. This time Olivia sat stiff and motionless on the side of her bed, avoiding Kitty's gaze. She sat down beside her and when she put her arm around her Olivia sagged and turned a tear–stained face towards her.

'Why did you *do* it, Kitty,' she said, sniffling and wiping away the tears, 'you must have *known* how it would hurt me! If you wanted him for yourself why did you encourage me? I don't understand!'

'My sweet, darling Olivia, I am so terribly sorry, I never intended to upset you, it is the very last thing I would ever want to do. You know what I am like, and have been like ever since we were children. I just got caught up in the moment and was blinded by the lure of a ride for the first time in what seems like ages as well as the chance to see Lionhurst! I am so impetuous and thoughtless sometimes but that's all it was, Olivia, I promise you!'

Olivia dried her eyes with a lace handkerchief and essayed a tremulous smile.

'If that is truly all it was, then … and I must confess that I do well know what you are like, Kitty! Ever since you were small you would rush into things without thinking! So all is now well between us.'

They embraced and Kitty made her way to her bedroom. She did feel relieved that the momentary rift was healed but felt a flush of shame at lying to her sister, for in her heart of hearts she could not deny that a lie is what it was.

'I *will* be strong for Olivia's sake!' she muttered to herself, startling a passing maid.

# VI

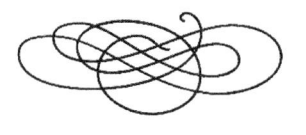

THE DAY OF THE BALL finally dawned and the household was soon in a frenzy of activity, toing and froing and hurrying, carrying, polishing, arranging and preparing. The usual tranquillity of country living was now punctuated by the crunch of wagon wheels on gravel, the snorting of draught horses, the groans of men carrying heavy loads and shouted orders and muttered curses as a seemingly endless river of deliveries flowed into Longton Manor until it seemed the house must burst at the seams. A dozen footmen from other great houses arrived one by one in the course of the day and were pounced upon and dragooned to receive instruction and assist wherever assistance was required. The individual Stricklands each had their assigned roles.

Sir Joshua took up his accustomed residence in the drawing room, the only departure from his habitual routine being an injunction delivered in the sternest possible manner by Lady Cecilia not to budge from his armchair, or derange any object in the room from its carefully chosen and polished state, and not to emerge from the room other than for sustenance and to change for the ball when the time came. The head of the household listened attentively and concluded that he had a firm grasp upon what was required of him, and was confident that the execution of his responsibilities was well within his capabilities.

Lady Cecilia was the eye of the storm, appearing here there and everywhere as if by magic, answering questions, pointing out insufficiencies that needed to be remedied, giving directions and making decisions about which mirrors to bring from which rooms to ensure sufficient reflection for the inordinate number of candles required, as well as innumerable matters large and small. The thought crossed her husband's mind that had Bonaparte but had the good fortune to have generals as fearsomely organised and decisive as Lady Cecilia, Wellington might have had a much more challenging time of it.

James was in town, discussing the purchase and future refurbishment of Lionhurst with the attentive Ernest Bagstock over a pint of ale in the Earl In Sunne tavern, where a plaque by the door boasted that it was the oldest such establishment not just in Wallstock but in the entire county. In addition to attending to the business of his future home, James was judiciously avoiding the madhouse at Longton Manor, thus killing two birds with one stone. He found Ernest to be both entertaining and extremely knowledgeable on all local matters, and that he was not afraid to voice his own opinions even if they were not in agreement with those of his companion. Thus over a very short acquaintance their encounters had become increasingly more like those of a nascent friendship rather of professional man and client.

Mr Bagstock took his leave from James to collect his chalks and make his way to Longton Manor for his rendezvous with the dance floor. Lady Cecilia received him with outpourings of effusive gratitude and while he prepared himself and laid out his chalks and a few preliminary sketches, the lady of the house summoned all the footmen and other servants to the entrance foyer, the only space other than the ballroom of sufficient size to accommodate them all.

'I want all of you to listen very carefully!' she began. 'That gentleman over there,' she continued, pointing her fan at Mr Bagshaw who was on his knees just making the first chalk strokes on the worn oak floor. 'is an artist whom we have been fortunate enough to persuade to decorate the dancefloor. I am sure at least some of you are familiar with this type of decoration. Now this is very important. Vital, in fact. Whenever any of you have cause to enter the ballroom you will only walk around the periphery, do you understand? I do not want a single swirl or line to be scuffed or smeared by a careless foot, is that clear? Do all of you understand?'

There was a general bobbing of heads and some muttered *Yes, My Lady*, and Lady Cecilia nodded with satisfaction.

'Excellent, and see that you remember! You are all dismissed, don't just stand about gawping, there is work to be done!'

She clapped her hands imperiously and the servitors shuffled off to resume their duties while Lady Cecilia headed for the kitchen to ensure there were no potential culinary disasters in the offing.

Olivia radiated a calming influence and drifted

almost unnoticed about the house, gently redirecting, assisting and correcting with the most pleasant manner so that all with whom she came in contact not only followed her instructions to the letter but were eager to do so. More than once Lady Cecilia found herself taken aback when the response to her instructions was that Miss Strickland had already identified the problem and taken the necessary measures. She passed the door to the ballroom and paused to watch Mr Bagshaw execute a dazzling twisted vine heavy with grapes, and without realising what she was doing she silently made her way to a chair in a far corner and watched him, fascinated by the ease and confidence with which he drew vines, leaves, branches and flowers, some wild as in nature and some as bouquets bound with fluttering ribbons.

He stood up and stretched, giving Olivia an opportunity to examine the man as well as his work. He was tall and slim with rebellious ginger hair over a pleasant and intelligent face. He turned and started when he saw her.

'Oh! Forgive me, I was quite unaware of your presence. You must be Miss Strickland, and I am Ernest Bagshaw, who foolishly succumbed to Miss Kitty's insistence that I decorate the dance floor. What do you think?'

He waved his hand vaguely towards the dance floor and Olivia stood up to get a better view. She stood there for quite some time as her eye was drawn from one chalk drawing to the next, each different but the overall effect like some fantastical garden bower.

'Oh, Mr Bagshaw! It is utterly beautiful! You are a true artist, and I can say that with some authority because I attempt to paint and fail, which allows me to appreciate your ability and finesse all the more.'

Her face clouded and she wrung her hands.

'To think that something so lovely is destined to be thoughtlessly and heedlessly trodden underfoot tonight, disregarded and unappreciated by most! It is so wrong!'

His face was wreathed in a smile at her adulation and without thinking he took her hand to guide her to a section of which he was particularly proud, and equally without thinking she allowed it. The two of them seemed to be in some manner of bubble that insulated them from the noisy goings on in the house as they talked about his art and the conversation gradually petered out until they were examining each other's faces as if they too were interesting works of art. The moment lasted no more than mere seconds before Lady Cecilia, having satisfied herself that all was progressing well in the kitchen, came bustling in and stopped dead in her tracks.

'My dear Mr Bagshaw! You have truly excelled yourself! This dance floor will make me the envy of all my guests and I have you to thank for it. Would you take it as a great impertinence if I were to ask you to the ball tonight? You must forgive me, but unfortunately I simply did not know you personally before today. Oh please do say yes, I beg you!'

He smilingly agreed and did not notice the happiness that flitted across Olivia's face before her mother dragged her off to deal with some task or other. He packed away his chalks and drawings and had his horse brought around and when he reached his apartments had the curious experience of being unable to remember anything beyond Olivia's smile and her praise, ringing with admiration and sincerity.

Alice meanwhile flitted about like some creature from a fairy tale missing only gossamer wings to complete the illusion, making ineffectual suggestions that the staff were astute and experienced enough to agree to and then ignore politely while she uttered little gasps of delight whenever her wide blue eyes fell upon things of beauty, which, given that the hall, the dining room and the ballroom were painstakingly and profusely decorated for the ball and replete with such objects, meant that her exhalations were practically continuous.

Kitty had made herself scarce in her special retreat in the sewing room, an oasis of calm in the pre–ball turbulence. From her favourite perch on the window seat she could watch the comings and goings from her eyrie with one eye while she did her best to focus on her latest acquisition, the novel *Zastrozzi*. Her expectations had been high – it was after all by Percy Bysshe Shelley, albeit hiding somewhat timidly behind his initials – but she was already beginning to regret her purchase and sympathise with his reticence to reveal himself. The plot seemed to her to be childish and lurid and she had only read three chapters when the sentence *"Would I had his heart reeking on my dagger, Signor!"* made her shake her head, yawn regretfully and put the slim volume on a bookshelf where she knew in her heart of hearts it would henceforth languish in well–deserved obscurity.

The hours crept inexorably by and the family convened at half past six for a light repast organised by Mrs Thrupp to sustain them until the ball's late supper.

'I do declare,' said Lady Cecilia as she pushed away

a half–eaten slice of boiled ham, 'I cannot eat a bite! I am far too agitated! Husband, promise me it will all go well!'

Sir Joshua was startled and discomfited by her demand, as well he might be considering that the consequence of his enforced confinement to the drawing room meant that he was blissfully ignorant of the many final preparations that had taken place that day. He did, however, know his wife well enough to know precisely what she required from him, and accordingly did not allow facts or his ignorance thereof to affect his reply in the slightest.

'Of *course* it will go well, my dear,' he said, and laid a soothing hand upon her arm. 'How could it possibly not? You have been exceedingly meticulous and have given every waking moment to the planning and executing of this venture, and of course you have had the inestimable comfort and advantage of the formidable Mrs Thrupp. I find it utterly inconceivable that it will be anything other than a triumph and the talk of the county for some considerable time to come.'

She squeezed his hand in gratitude and allowed herself to reflect with uncritical complacency that her husband's words were no more and no less than the literal truth.

Sir Joshua, James and the ladies of the house then retired to their respective rooms, the latter still agonising over the selection of their gowns despite there now being no possibility of altering their choices.

The sun sank below the horizon shortly before the clock struck half past seven, and darkness fell with what seemed to Lady Cecilia and her daughters to be interminable slowness. James and Kitty had completed their sartorial transformations and found themselves alone in the drawing room, gazing out of the tall windows as the last pink tinges faded from the clouds and the sky underwent its inexorable transformation from day to night.

'It is a magical time of day, is it not.' James said softly. 'But it is so majestically slow here! In India there was but a short interval between the setting of the sun and complete darkness. Mrs Khambata used to say it was a time when the veils that separate us from other worlds are at their thinnest, and indeed, even here there is an accompanying hush that seems to envelop everything as we wait for the inevitable darkness.'

His brow furrowed and his eyes took on a faraway look, prompting Kitty to ask whether he was thinking about his lady tutor. He passed his hands over his eyes and looked at her sadly.

'Yes, you are correct. Is reading minds one of your hidden talents?'

'You had a faraway look in your eyes and your mind had clearly travelled to a faraway place,' she replied. 'I saw a similar sadness when you spoke of her before. Will you tell me what happened to her?'

His jaw clamped and it was as if he was having difficulty speaking.

'She died!' He pressed out the words as if with great effort and she saw that his fists were balled so tightly that the knuckles were white.

'Please tell me what happened?' she said softly and he took a pace back while he rubbed the side of his head, and in the light of the candelabra next to which he stood she really took note for the first time of his scar, long healed but of a peculiar shape, as he abstractedly pushed back his hair with his hand.

'Enough, I beg you!' His voice was strained and filled with an unfocussed anger. 'I cannot tell you because I *cannot remember!* Are you satisfied now!'

He turned and marched rigidly out into the hallway without a backward glance. Kitty followed him to the door and saw that he had gone outside and was standing motionless in the driveway. Two footmen appeared with flaming torches and positioned themselves on either side of the main entrance while others formed orderly lines on either side of the marble steps leading to the entrance while yet more waited in the hallway, ready to relieve guests of their hats, canes, cloaks or any other garments and paraphernalia from which they might wish to be unburdened. Outside on the drive two more waited patiently, ready to leap into action to lower carriage steps and open carriage doors and render assistance to those alighting where necessary, whereupon Jackson appeared, dignified under a carefully powdered wig and wearing a splendid coat of gold brocade that would not have looked out of place in the court of the Sun King himself.

All that needed to be done and could be done, had been done. Every person high and low at Longton Manor was at their post and silence fell, broken only by the distant dissonances of the musicians tuning their instruments in the ballroom and the crackling of the torches. All at once the players were done, apparently satisfied with their tuning and when silence returned all eyes turned with involuntary anticipation to the distant entrance gates, freshly repainted in shiny black and gold, and waited in the hush for the first carriages to appear between them.

# VII

FIRST TO ARRIVE was Lady Tremayne, widow of the late Viscount Tremayne and one of the Strickland's closest neighbours. She was a thickset woman of middle years, amiable and jolly, and it was whispered with a degree of cruel amusement that she appeared markedly jollier since her dour husband had been elevated from earthly to celestial aristocracy. She was greeted warmly by the Strickland family, introduced to James and as she used a stick because of an arthritic hip was ushered into the drawing room to wait in comfort where she and Lady Cecilia chatted animatedly until the next carriage arrived.

Lady Cecilia had gone to some lengths to ensure that some of the more elevated of her friends and acquaintances would arrive somewhat earlier than usual, in order to avert the potential disaster of their illustrious guests arriving and being led into an empty house. Once most of them had arrived the noise level gradually rose as they reacquainted themselves with each other and appreciatively sampled Sir Joshua's champagne, when a footman ran up to him and Lady Cecilia and deferentially but urgently interrupted their conversation.

'Begging your pardon Sir, my Lady, but Mr Jackson begs to inform you that a coach displaying the arms of the Earl of Wallstock is entering the estate at this very moment.'

With a muttered 'Thank You' Sir Joshua and his wife straightened their clothing without being aware of doing so and hurried outside while attempting to strike a balance between speed and dignity and it is a credit to their long experience of society functions that in this endeavour they largely succeeded.

The gleaming black and yellow coach bore the Earl's coat of arms on the door and the coachman wore a smart blue cloak and yellow top hat adorned with a jaunty blue plume. A footmen ran to attend it and the opened door first disgorged Lady Georgina, Dowager Countess of Wallstock, resplendent in a grey silk ballgown and an emerald green cloak with collar and cuffs of white mink, her impressively coiffed confection of silvery hair surmounted by an elaborate tiara of diamonds and emeralds that teetered uneasily on the brink of ostentation from which it was saved only by the elevated rank of its wearer. She waited for her son to alight and arm in arm followed Jackson, who bowed low and indicated with a stately sweep of his arm that they should follow him. Hurrying to keep up with them came the Earl's younger brother and sister, the former a slim young man in his early twenties and by contrast to his brother and two female relatives, dressed with relative simplicity in white hose and a deep blue jacket. His sister's gown of watered silk shimmered subtly from blue to turquoise as she moved, and her blonde hair while simply curled and prepared was crowned by a restrained tiara of diamonds and blue sapphires, if the word restrained may be used in such a context, relatively modest in both size and design.

The Earl himself was one of that tribe of immediately identifiable Anglo–Saxons with regular, square–jawed features, blue eyes and yellow–blond hair that appears immediately attractive and trustworthy at first acquaintance. It is only upon closer inspection, were one to succeed in brushing aside the veils of amiability and bonhomie with which he cloaked himself, that his eyes might at some point allow an astute observer a glimpse of the inner man. They crinkled obediently in concert with an easy and well–practised open grin. However to inspect them with analytic purpose was to gaze through clear blue windows untrammelled by genuine feeling or emotion and lacking anything real or warm or human, into an infinity of nothing behind them. But the sycophantic adulation with which men of his status were generally received meant that such penetrating observation was indeed a thing of considerable rarity.

After effusive greetings from Sir Joshua and introductions between the two families had been completed the Wallstocks strolled unhurriedly to the ballroom, graciously accepting glasses of champagne from silver trays proffered by attentive footmen. The hum of conversation punctuated by occasional bursts of laughter petered out momentarily as this most august family of the county entered, but the other guests quickly caught themselves and avoided unseemly staring while they swiftly resumed their previous exchanges and to everyone's relief the potentially awkward moment passed in an instant and all reverted to normal.

By now all the guests had arrived and changed their shoes from those they had travelled in to pumps and slippers suitable for dancing. Lady Cecilia raised a discreet eyebrow when she caught Jackson's eye, and after equally discreetly glancing at a sheet of paper unobtrusively extracted from his coat pocket, permitted himself what could almost have been deemed a smile, and nodded imperceptibly. Thus relieved and now in possession of the knowledge that all upon the guest list were present and accounted for, Lady Cecilia looked around the ballroom with some satisfaction at the many mirrors cannibalised from all over the house and hung artfully around the room to reflect and multiply the glow from a substantial central chandelier and numerous candelabra dotted about the periphery, bathing the guests in the lambent and flattering light of dozens of six–hour candles. Sir Joshua's talents in obtaining sufficient supplies of champagne despite the exorbitant cost and difficulty of finding sufficient quantities of it as a consequence of the regrettable inconvenience of the war with France were clearly appreciated by one and all, and he was especially gratified to overhear even Lady Wallstock remarking on its satisfactory quality.

While Alice flitted about the room with the air of a happy butterfly sampling new varieties of nectar, her parents carefully circulated and made sure to include all the guests in their peregrinations, serving the dual purpose of ensuring that no guest would feel neglected, and to graciously absorb the many envy–tinged compliments on having managed to snare guests such as the Crasmeres. Kitty, Olivia and James stood together observing rather than participating in the festivities.

'I do believe Mama is asking Lady Wallstock to call the first dance,' said Olivia, having observed her mother talking animatedly with the said lady. 'But I fear she has declined – graciously, by the look of it – and told Mama she should take on that honour herself.'

'I do believe you are correct,' said Kitty, 'but what is this now?'

The Earl of Wallstock was making his way purposefully towards their little group, and both women had to admit that he cut a rather fine and handsome figure in an exquisite vest of silver brocade set off by snowy linen and an embroidered black velvet jacket. He stopped in front of Kitty and bowed his head a finely judged fraction, just sufficient to indicate an agreeable greeting but not in any way to suggest subservience.

'My dear Madam, I do believe the first dance is about to be called and would be grateful if you would do me the honour of sharing it with me.'

Kitty was lost for words but the Earl took her inarticulacy for assent and held out his arm. What was she to do? If she made an excuse she would not only be snubbing the head of the pre–eminent family of the county, but etiquette would demand that if she refused the first dance she would be barred from dancing for the rest of the ball.

'Thank you, Lord Crasmere, this is most unexpected!'

'I cannot imagine why,' he replied with a boyish grin. 'You are not only the most attractive woman in the room, but, I suspect, the most intelligent. So in future I suggest you might care to adjust your expectations upwards!'

Lady Cecilia duly called a longways Country Dance and they took their positions, waiting patiently for the lines to form and arrange themselves in an orderly fashion before the musicians struck up a lively tune and the dancers furthest from them took the first steps.

'I understand you were recently in India, my Lord,' said Kitty as they waited for the dance to reach them and their cue to begin.

'As, so I have been told, was your cousin over there, dancing with your charming sister. Alas I do not believe our paths crossed but that is hardly surprising given the enormity of the sub–continent and the many thousands of us British out there.'

'Yes, yes of course, you are quite right, how absurd of me! It is as if I were to have the expectation that everyone in the Home Counties was somehow personally acquainted with each other!'

His teeth were very even and very white and displayed frequently with a disarming grin attractively seasoned with a soupçon of roguishness. Their turn in the dance soon reached them and after a few moments Kitty had to admit that he was an excellent dancer, nimble and inventive and she supposed it was to be expected as the family could certainly afford the finest dance masters. She could not help but notice his square jaw, the symmetry of his features, the deep blue of his eyes and his general air of confidence and athleticism. She spied James dancing with Olivia and noted that while perfectly competent he could not match her partner's effortless expertise, but that did not prevent Olivia from looking radiantly happy as they swirled and linked arms. It seemed to Kitty that James frequently glanced her way and was flattered until she realised to her surprise that it was not her but her partner who was his focus. She shook off her momentary puzzlement and returned her attentions to keeping up with the Earl.

They were both out of breath by the time the dance ended and her partner kissed her hand and made a sweeping courtly bow before suggesting they avail themselves of refreshment as he spied some footmen circulating with trays of iced punch as well as glasses of champagne. She had expected him to move on to mingle with others but the Earl remained by her side, amusing her with anecdotes of the eccentric tenants on their estate and making Kitty very slightly uncomfortable as he attributed absurd statements to them and mimicked their broad country accents and lack of education with deadly accuracy. She suppressed the small voice that found these tales rather mean and condescending, but laughed despite herself. He was a good looking aristocrat, beautifully dressed, handsome, an exceptional dancer and an amusing raconteur, and even in the very short time since he first spoke to her she could feel herself being unwillingly drawn to him.

Perhaps it was a combination of the punch – strongly fortified with rum, brandy and wine – and his engaging comportment that made her speak in a manner that she would never otherwise have contemplated upon such short acquaintance.

'Forgive me for being forward, but it must have been very hard for you, Sir, to lose not only your father as well as your brother in such short order, *and* to have the responsibility of the Earldom thrust upon you so unexpectedly.'

For a fleeting moment her amiable dancing companion's easy charm disappeared and he fixed her with a piercing, rapier–like gaze so hard and uncompromising that it made her breath catch in her throat but then the moment passed and he smiled.

'You are *most* forward, Madam,' he said evenly, 'but I see that your sympathy is genuine and not mere idle curiosity, so I will excuse it on this occasion. However I do not choose to discuss such intimate personal matters upon such brief acquaintance. Please forgive me in turn, I see that Mama is being bored to death by Lady Tremayne and is in dire need of rescue.'

He bowed perfunctorily and walked away, leaving Kitty with the unpleasant and unaccustomed sense of being an inferior who had been coldly reprimanded and dismissed. Her sisters hurried over and bombarded her with questions.

'What an honour for the Earl to choose you for the first dance!'

'Oh he is *so* handsome, Kitty! I am surprised you did not swoon at his attentions!'

'What did you talk about? What did he say?'

'He is such an accomplished dancer, is he not!'

Kitty laughed and brushed them off, her uneasiness about her last exchange with the Earl superseded by taking innocent pleasure in the garrulously animated enjoyment of her sisters. Moments later Lady Cecilia joined them and favoured Kitty with an arch smile.

'*Well*, my darling, you are a dark horse indeed, are you not! Capturing our most illustrious guest in less time than it takes to tell! Who would have thought you had it in you!'

She squeezed Kitty's arm approvingly and hurried off to confer with the musicians for the next dance. Kitty danced once with James whose performance was perfunctory, his conversation withdrawn and practically monosyllabic, and lastly with the Honourable Frederick Crasmere, the youngest sibling, a quietly pleasant young man with a recognisable family resemblance to his older brother, though rendered slimmer, softer and less assertive. But it was Alice who danced with him most often and to whom his eyes kept straying. Mr Bagshaw was clearly somewhat ill at ease with the ball, but when James retired from the dance floor Olivia sought him out and when the next dance was called, he hesitantly asked her and she accepted. He was not an accomplished dancer but acquitted himself adequately, and Olivia did not mind at all. It was only afterwards that it struck her how much she had enjoyed his lively conversation, only minutes after dancing with James.

After more dancing and a lavish supper the ball began to break up in the early hours of the morning when the Dowager Countess pleaded fatigue and summoned her coach, taking her brood with her. Amidst the farewells and thanks and compliments and wishes for a safe journey back to Wraxton Place, the Earl took Kitty's hand and manoeuvred her away from the melee of guests in the hallway.

'It has been an excellent and most enjoyable ball, Madam, Sir Joshua and Lady Cecilia are to be congratulated, but by far the greatest pleasure has been that of making your acquaintance. I do hope to get to know you better and look forward to seeing you again in the near future.'

The Stricklands followed the Crasmeres out to their carriage and waved as it crunched off across the gravel into the night. The family hurried back inside to see to the remaining guests who were preparing to leave, but Kitty lingered for a moment. She had observed that as the Earl turned his face towards the flickering light of the torches being held by footmen, her cousin James seemed to suffer a sudden affliction and staggered momentarily until he was able to steady himself against a wall. Most puzzling of all was his expression of wide–eyed shock. All this happened in a matter of seconds before he managed to collect himself and follow the others inside. Kitty was fairly certain that only she had noticed the strange moment, for by then the others had turned away to re–enter the house. In a pause between departing guests she laid a gentle hand on her step–cousin's arm.

'My dear cousin, are you ill? It seemed to me that you were briefly unwell just now as the Crasmeres were departing.'

She was unprepared for the hunted look on his face as he stammered that he was absolutely fine, that it was no more than a glass too many of champagne and punch and the cool night air after the warmth of the ballroom. She did not believe him for a moment but was at a loss as to how to get him to open up to her. Later, when all the guests had gone Kitty was in her bedroom seated at her dressing table in her sleeping shift, absent–mindedly brushing her hair when Lady Cecilia knocked and entered. She sat on the bed, patted the covers and took Kitty's hand when she sat down beside her.

'I am *so* happy, my child!' she said, and her

daughter nodded.

'Yes, Mama, it was a triumph! Everything went so well, the music, the decorations, the dances, the food, Papa's champagne … ' her voice petered out as her mother shook her head emphatically.

'Kitty, Kitty, Kitty! I *do* utterly despair of you sometimes! That is not what I meant *at all!* Yes I am naturally gratified that it all went off so well but what I meant was you and Lord Crasmere! What an honour! It is clear he has taken a liking to you, that was patently obvious to everyone! Oh, Kitty! Never in my most optimistic imaginings could I have conceived of you married to the Earl of Wallstock! A Countess! And Alice married to his younger brother!'

She clapped her hands in joy and in her mind's eye was clearly already seeing and planning the weddings and the happy times to come that would see her daughters well taken care of and launched into futures not only secure and comfortable but of elevated status.

'And what of Olivia?' asked Kitty in disbelief. 'There are only two male Crasmeres available, Mama, so is she perhaps to marry Lady Emilia?'

'Oh Kitty!' said her mother exasperatedly, wagging an admonishing finger at her. 'This is a very serious matter! I see a glorious future for my daughters taking shape and all you can do is say the most ridiculous things! Sometimes I think you do it just to vex me! Of *course* Olivia will marry James, surely you must have noticed how frequently they are in each other's company of late?'

Kitty was lost for words at the presumptuousness of her mother's fantasies and did her best to ignore the uncomfortable stab of an emotion she would not let herself believe was jealousy at the mention of James.

'Mama! You are building castles upon the sand! I had a dance and a conversation and that is *all* and I have no intention *whatsoever* of marrying the Earl of Wallstock even in the *extremely* unlikely event that he was to take such a madcap notion into his head!'

Lady Cecilia tenderly kissed her youngest daughter on the forehead and rose to leave.

'It is late and we have all had a surfeit of excitement tonight,' she said in a conciliatory manner. 'I am sure that in the light of day you will see that what I wish for the three of you is the best outcome for your futures that we could possibly hope for. Sleep well, my darling. Good night.'

She closed the door behind her and Kitty threw herself onto the bed and stared at the dancing patterns the flickering candles made on the ceiling. She blew them out and slid under the covers and tried to make herself comfortable and ready to welcome sleep, but the arms of Morpheus stubbornly refused to enfold her. There was something troubling behind the superficial attractiveness of the Earl, something maddeningly elusive no matter how often she turned it over and over and re–examined every moment of their encounters at the ball.

True, he had been uncompromising in refusing to respond to her sympathy and open himself to her, but on the other hand he had done it in a manner that was not explicitly rude and that somewhat mitigated the severity of the rejection. But the more she replayed the exchange in her mind the more certain she became that beneath the cold assertion of his right to privacy had been something else. And that the something else had been *fear*. After an hour of fruitlessly chasing sleep she gave up and determined to go downstairs in the hope that a little distraction would dispel whatever was keeping her awake. She got up, wrapped herself in a robe and with no clear plan in mind ventured out into the darkened house, descended the staircase and headed towards the drawing room.

The house was absolutely silent and all the servants had gone to bed, no doubt exhausted by the demands of the ball, so she was surprised to see a faint light under the drawing room door and when she entered saw by the light of a single candle on a side table James slumped in Papa's armchair with his head in his hands. He looked up as she closed the door behind her and she glimpsed something in his expression just before it was supplanted by surprise at seeing her, something that seemed as best she could tell to be an unsettling and inexplicable amalgam of fury and despair.

'Kitty! What on earth are you doing here at this hour?'

'I might well ask you the same question, James! I could not sleep and came down seeking some diversion to pass the time until sleep finally finds me. Is it the same with you?'

'It is indeed, Kitty, precisely so. I could not sleep either.'

She sat on the sofa and leaned forward.

'Dear James, I am certain there is something that is deeply troubling you, and that when we spoke earlier it had nothing whatsoever to do with champagne or punch or warmth or cool night air. Will you not tell me what troubles you? Whatever it is, you must know that I am no gossip and your secret would be completely safe with me.'

He stared at her for what seemed an inordinate amount of time before slumping back in his armchair.

'Oh Kitty! I cannot! Something once happened, it is true, but … I am in some confusion as to the true nature of it, and it would be wrong to burden you with things only half–remembered, which, were they to prove to be true, are terrible indeed. I will tell you when I am certain, dear cousin. Until then, that is all I can say.'

He hesitated before continuing and leaned forward and to her surprise took her hand in his.

'Dear Kitty, this may sound strange but I swear upon my honour that what I am about to say is motivated by nothing else but my concern for your wellbeing. That is my *sole* consideration. Do not, I beg you, allow yourself to be drawn too close to the Earl of Wallstock. I could see clearly that he has you in his sights and I fear for you, were you to permit him to persuade you to … greater closeness.'

Kitty was speechless at her cousin's declaration, delivered as it was with the utmost seriousness and gravity.

'James! Whatever can you mean? What an extremely odd thing to say to me! What *possible* meaning am I to attach to such utterances! In fact, despite the affection I have for you, how dare you presume to tell me what I should or should not do! I am truly astonished! I encounter you here, both of us fugitives from insomnolence, I see that something is troubling you and offer to share your troubles, and in return you speak as though you were my father with a right to tell me who I should or should not befriend! I am quite at a loss to explain your behaviour. Good night!'

Shaking her head she stalked out of the room and went upstairs to bed. Despite her displeasure at James' extraordinary remarks she soon fell asleep and dreamed that she was being whirled around the dance floor faster and faster by a shadowy figure who would not stop despite her increasingly desperate cries.

# VIII

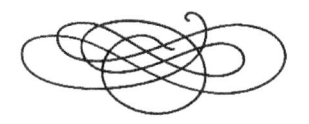

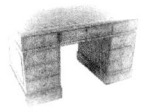

THE DAY AFTER the ball dawned bright and fair and when Alice said she had arranged to meet the Earl's sister Lady Emilia at Bartlett's Tea Rooms that afternoon, Kitty decided to accompany her for want of anything better to do. She was not only at something of a loose end and experiencing a certain feeling of lassitude in the wake of the excitement of the ball but, as James appeared briefly for breakfast and clearly avoided engaging with her and disappeared soon afterwards, she was more than content to return the compliment.

Kitty let Alice's endless chatter wash over her amidst the gentle breeze and the warm country smell of freshly cut hay and the clip–clop of the horses' hooves that all lulled her into a semi–torpor as the phaeton carried them sedately to Wallstock. Once there Alice insisted they first visit Whittaker's Emporium to ascertain whether any more fashions had arrived since scrutinising them when they were having their gowns made for the ball. It was only when Kitty pointed to the ornate clock on the Emporium's wall that Alice realised the appointed hour was upon them and tore herself reluctantly from the latest catalogues and they hurried down the pavement to the tea rooms.

Lady Emilia had only just arrived and they chose a table by a bay window from which they could watch the world (or such minuscule fraction of it as was present in Wallstock) go by. After they had chosen their tea and a plate of cucumber sandwiches Alice and Lady Emilia animatedly discussed the latest offerings at Whittaker's and the distressing shortage of French lace which they deemed to be a most inconsiderate and very low and ungentlemanly tactic on the part of Bonaparte. In the meanwhile Kitty amused herself by observing the distorted images of passers–by in the roundels of crown glass that dotted the bay window. She was startled when Lady Emilia gently placed an expensively gloved hand on her arm with a smile.

'You Strickland ladies must have some special secret, Kitty – I do hope you don't mind me calling you Kitty, I do so *detest* the formality to which our station in life attempts to condemn us, and you must call me Emilia, now that the two of you have captivated *both* my brothers, no mean feat, I assure you. Poor Frederick was heard to remark that Miss Alice was both pretty *and* amiable, which for him is the equivalent of a long and ardent speech! And as for Hugo ... well let us say he was very complimentary about you, Kitty, very complimentary indeed!'

She laughed and clapped her hands before daintily sipping her tea.

'I see I have made both of you blush! I am sorry, it

was perhaps just the *slightest* bit indelicate on my part to mention it, but I thought you should know and was simply unable to resist! Mmmm, these sandwiches are really very good indeed! Much more delicate than our poor Cook's efforts at Wraxton Place! I must try and remember to speak to her about it. We may have to order another plate before long!'

Lady Emilia's utterances invariably seemed to require an exclamation mark to complete them and when Alice pressed her excitedly for more details and Lady Emilia offered up exhaustive analyses of Frederick's most insignificant comments Kitty again drifted mentally and resumed her idle observance of the High Street. Diagonally across the road some hundred yards further along was the substantial and well–kept house of Dr Astley, who at that very moment emerged with James and as on the previous occasion she had observed them, shook hands most cordially before James walked away until he was out of sight.

'I am *so* sorry, you must forgive me, I have just recalled an errand I am afraid I am obliged to fulfil,' she said. 'I am sure the two of you have many things to discuss and I will in any case be back shortly.'

They smiled briefly in acknowledgement and Lady Emilia immediately continued her expositions while Alice hung breathlessly upon every word. Kitty made her way across the road to the doctor's residence and used the brass door knocker to announce her presence. A maid opened the door and ushered her into a sparsely but tastefully furnished parlour, saying that the doctor would be with her in a moment. As promised he appeared moments later via a side door through which she glimpsed a large desk and an examination table.

'Miss Kitty! I am so sorry to have kept you waiting, please forgive me, but I was just updating my notes on my previous patient. At my age I have learned that it is best to record such matters while the memory is still fresh!' He laughed self–deprecatingly. 'First of all allow me to say what a splendid ball your family put on at Longton Manor, it was a truly enjoyable evening and while I have of course written them a note of thanks, I would be most grateful if you would kindly personally convey my gratitude for the invitation to your parents. And while it goes without saying that it is always a pleasure to encounter you, dear lady, I do hope it is not some serious malady that brings you to me! I always say that my favourite patients are the ones I never see! Please, do come in.'

He closed the door and Kitty sat on a comfortably padded chair opposite him at his desk. He wrote a few lines on a sheet of paper and put it into a file which he closed and pushed to one side before sitting back and steepling his fingers. He was a tall, distinguished looking man, impeccably but not flashily dressed with a kind and intelligent face framed by a mane of silver hair that altogether invited trust and confidences.

'You have my full attention, Madam. Please proceed and tell me why you have come to see me.'

Kitty had not really thought through what precisely she was going to say and desperately searched her mind for some symptom credible enough to justify her visit while at the same time sufficiently mild and vague to allow her to escape. What had she been thinking? It was her curse, she thought to herself, to speak and act before considering all the consequences, but unfortunately that was not a malady one could present to a doctor. She returned to the present to see Dr Astley waiting patiently with slightly raised eyebrows, no doubt accustomed to patients who had difficulty in articulating symptoms often of a very personal and intimate nature.

'Oh, it is nothing, really,' she finally said, attempting to gain some additional time to allow herself to think. 'I feel rather foolish to bother you with what is no more than … an occasional dizziness, very occasional, and it usually passes swiftly,' she ended, pleased that inspiration had rescued her at the eleventh hour. There was a knock on the door and when the doctor called out 'I am with a patient!' the knocking became louder and the maid opened the door.

'Begging your pardon, Sir, Miss, but a messenger has come with urgent news that Mrs Upton's waters have done broke and they do beg you to attend them at your very earliest convenience. I have asked the boy to tell the stables to saddle your horse and bring it to the door as swiftly as possible.'

'Very good, Mary, you have done well, thank you. Give the lad tuppence and I will be there momentarily.'

He threw his hands up regretfully and retrieved his fashionable tall–crowned beaver hat from a stand before picking up his voluminous medical bag.

'I am most awfully sorry, Miss Kitty, but the lady in question has had considerable difficulties with her previous births so I dare not delay even for a moment and must attend urgently. Forgive me for saying so, but from the sound of it your malady appears somewhat less urgent in nature, so perhaps you would be kind enough to make another appointment with Mary.'

An audacious plan sprung ready formed into Kitty's mind and true to her nature she followed it instantly and unhesitatingly. She stood up to take Dr Astley's proffered hand and staggered, putting a hand to her head and sinking back onto her chair.

'Oh forgive me, dear Dr Astley, but it is one of those episodes I was describing to you! How inopportune! Please do go, the unfortunate lady is clearly in greater need of you! If you would indulge me and be kind enough to inform your maid to allow me to sit here quietly for a few minutes to collect myself that would be a great kindness.'

'Of course, of course, the office is at your disposal, please take as much time as you require! Goodbye, Madam, and remember to make another appointment when you can be assured of my undivided attention.'

The neighing of a horse outside galvanised him and he strode to the door, pausing only to have a few words with the maid before closing the door behind him. Kitty waited until the sound of the departing horse's hooves had diminished to nothing and opened the door a crack, but the maid was nowhere to be seen. She closed it carefully and hurried around to the doctor's side of the desk, picked up the file he had closed when she arrived and quickly went back to the chair upon which she had been sitting. With both ears straining to hear the maid's approach she ran her eyes over the sheets of paper in the file, mentally giving thanks to Aesculapius and all the other gods of medicine that Dr Astley wrote with a beautifully legible hand, in marked contrast to so many others of his fellow practitioners.

> *Subject : James Alexander Strickland*
> *Age : 27*
> *Address : Longton Manor*
> *Other : Adoptive (?) Nephew to Sir Joshua Strickland*

*The subject is only recently returned from the Indian sub–continent, in which place he lived with and was brought up by his stepfather from an early age following the death of his mother, Mr Strickland's sister–in–law, and his father in a coaching accident. He was therefore no blood relative but nonetheless – to his great credit – Mr Strickland treated him in every way as if he were his own son and took him to India when his wife died, eventually taking him into his trading enterprise as a partner when the lad was old enough and made him his sole heir. Would that more men in his position would behave thus honourably!*

*A thorough initial physical examination shows him to be in excellent health and exhibiting no signs of any of the exotic maladies either present or past that some returnees from the Far East carry back with them as unwanted souvenirs, and he confirms that he was lucky enough to have escaped these while growing up. His stepfather died recently which occasioned the disposal of all the family business and property in India and his eventual return to these shores.*

Kitty clicked her tongue in irritation as she sped through the first paragraphs which largely only contained information of which she was already aware.

*It has become clear to me that something is burdening*

*this young man's mind, and that <u>most</u> unusually he cannot pinpoint the matter, and I can only conclude he is suffering from what the Frenchman* Sauvages *defined as a medical disorder that he named* Amnesia.

*His examination did reveal a scar approximately two inches in length with evidence of somewhat crude stitching, no doubt by a local garrison doctor more accustomed to the necessity for speed in dealing with battlefield wounds than aesthetics. Careful closer examination reveals some – albeit very slight – deformity of the underlying bone beneath the scar, leading me to conclude that he suffered a blow of some considerable force sufficient to crack the skull where the affected area has now thankfully knitted together and effectively repaired itself. This in turn has led me to two possible conclusions.*

1. *The blow occasioned some localised damage to the brain, leading to a small, very particular loss of memory with no other observable side effects.*
2. *The loss of memory may well be tied to whatever traumatic event occasioned the injury, and it is the horror of the event <u>rather than the consequence of the injury itself</u> that is the root cause of the problem.*

*As there is plainly little I can do in the first case, I have concentrated my efforts on the second possibility, as – `if this is indeed the case – <u>the memory may well still be there,</u> merely isolated and suppressed due to an understandable unwillingness to relive the traumatic event.*

*I have elicited some small success in that we have managed to narrow down the period in time during which this event must have taken place, and I have taken an indirect rather than a head-on approach. In order to facilitate this process I have studied the theories of the German physician Franz Mesmer, and while his beliefs regarding its nature which he terms 'animal magnetism' are increasingly discredited by many eminent physicians these days, few would argue with the fact that the actual mechanism of mesmerism or hypnosis, whatever the truth of it's exact nature, can on occasion achieve remarkable results.*

Kitty was fascinated and picked up the second sheet and as it was headed with today's date she concluded it must be the one she had seen Dr Astley writing just before he left, an assumption confirmed by a smudge of not yet fully dried ink on her finger. She hurriedly read on.

*The subject arrived today without an appointment and was in a highly agitated state. Once I was able to somewhat calm him he confided that he had met an individual at the ball whom he was convinced had been involved in the problematic event that had caused his amnesia. And further, that while he could still recall nothing else of it, he was adamant that this person had played some unpleasant part. He has agreed to allow me to attempt to unlock his memories using Mesmer's techniques, and I have accordingly asked him to make an appointment after next week, as I will be in London for a few days.*

Kitty was in turmoil but the approaching sound of the maid's stout footwear clumping on the floorboards allowed her just enough time to reinstate the papers in the file and replace it on the other side of the desk, and by the time Mary entered she was sitting slumped in her chair and smiled wanly at the girl.

'Are you all right, Miss?' she asked and Kitty assured her she was feeling much better and was just preparing to leave. Once outside she saw to her enormous relief that Alice and Lady Emilia had ended their gossipy tea and were standing on the pavement saying their farewells. She joined them, apologised for her absence and said goodbye to Lady Emilia. Arm in arm the two sisters made their way to where Tom was waiting patiently with the phaeton, boarded it and went home. Alice tried to ascertain what Kitty's fictitious errand had been, but eventually gave up in a huff after receiving only non–committal and monosyllabic responses.

Kitty could only think of what she had discovered at Dr Astley's surgery and little else and had endless questions whirling around maddeningly in her head like a swarm of annoying bees. After the strong reaction she had observed when James saw the Earl's face as he mounted his coach, she was certain it could be no other to whom the doctor's notes referred. And of course there was James' unsettlingly strange behaviour and offensive words later last night in the Drawing Room.

For Kitty the following days passed in a ferment of mounting frustration at not being able to find out more. On top of that the sight of James and Olivia occasionally strolling in the gardens and admiring Ned's dazzling displays of roses made her say 'Thank God she doesn't ride,' under her breath and feel immediately ashamed and contrite at such a selfish thought. It was, after all no more than her own doing and what she had decided to try and achieve for Olivia.

The day was grey and that peculiarly cheerless English form of rain we call drizzle had settled in and showed no sign of moving on. James was out with his newfound friend and Man Friday Ernest Bagstock, busy with the purchase and renovation plans for Lionhurst while the rest of the Strickland family were sitting in the Drawing Room variously occupied. Sir Joshua was as always happily buried deep in the folds of his beloved Times. Kitty and Olivia sat by the windows, reading. Kitty sighed and closed her book, carefully placing a bookmark. It was *Forest of Montalbano* by Catherine Cuthbertson, a much easier read than the truly awful *Zastrozzi* but the frequency with which its female characters swooned and fainted was beginning to become tiresome and vexatious to her. Olivia was deeply immersed in Walter Scott's *The Lady of the Lake* while Alice was attempting embroidery, an activity punctuated by yelps and growls of irritation as she pricked her finger and constantly had to undo and redo stitches. Lady Cecilia sat absently fanning herself, occasionally emerging from her unknowable but easily guessable thoughts to cast a fond and complacent eye over her family before lapsing into her reverie.

There was a knock at the door and Jackson proffered a letter on a silver salver. She thanked him and sat bolt upright when she saw that the envelope bore the unmistakeable blue and yellow coat of arms of the Earl of Wallstock. She called for a knife and carefully dislodged the wax seal, all the while uttering disjointed phrases of delight. Once she had read it she held it aloft in much the same way as Moses might have held up the stone tablets with the Ten Commandments.

'Husband! Daughters! The note is from the Dowager Countess of Wallstock and – I can scarcely credit it – we are invited to tea at Wraxton Place! The day after tomorrow! All of us, including James!'

She clutched the letter to her bosom and closed her eyes as if in transports of ecstasy.

'Oh how jealous they will all be!' she said with gleeful satisfaction.

'Whom do you mean, mother?' asked Kitty innocently, suppressing a smile.

'Why, every single lady in this part of the county with marriageable daughters, of course!' replied her mother impatiently, rising to the bait as Kitty knew she would.

'Only *two days!* Oh my dears, we have much work to do! Jackson! Ah, there you are, and yet again I find myself welcoming your otherwise deplorable habit of lurking so perhaps I should simply resign myself to it! I will write a response to send to Wraxton Place with all speed, so make sure there is someone ready to take it there. Oh, and kindly retrieve Sir Joshua's brown coat, you know, the one with the velvet collar and cuffs, and ask Mrs Thrupp to ensure it is clean and free of stains. And that his best boots are gleaming, *gleaming*, do you hear me?'

# IX

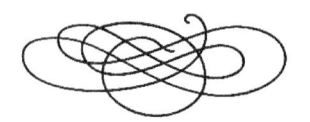

AS THE PHAETON would not bear more than two Stricklands in comfort and the landau had not seen much recent use, Tom and Ned were instructed to inspect it thoroughly for roadworthiness and to touch up the paintwork and especially the modest Strickland arms on the doors with its motto of *Honestas est Omne*, Honesty is All, as well as to thoroughly polish every part of it. It would be pulled by Bella and Balthazar, who though primarily riding horses, had for reasons of economy been used as occasional carriage horses with sufficient frequency to be reliable as well as unresentfully accustomed to their secondary role.

The big day dawned with yet more pleasing blue skies for which Lady Cecilia offered up a heartfelt prayer of thanks, as there is little a lady can do to protect the exquisite daintiness of her shoes and the ruffled perfection of her dress hems in the face of pouring rain and its inevitable clinging companion mud, those twin despoilers of perfection and elegance that lie in wait in the exposed no man's land between carriages and the sanctuary of doorways. The two conveyances drew up in the driveway before the front door and Sir Joshua and Lady Cecilia paused to admire the newly repainted purple and blue Strickland arms on the landau doors before boarding the phaeton, while James and the three daughters of the house arranged themselves in the landau. Ned and Tom had been outfitted in newly purchased caped blue overcoats with purple collars and trim, but to Lady Cecilia's chagrin Sir Joshua had drawn the line at matching headgear and they wore simple black top hats.

'Enough is enough, dear lady,' he had said. 'They were both in sore need of new coats in any case, so I did not begrudge that necessary expense. However, do let us try and remember that we are merely visiting our neighbours, and while it is true that they are above us in station, the occasion is, after all, nothing more than an invitation to tea. I doubt they will even see Ned and Tom at all, and should they do so, I further doubt that the sight of their black hats will destroy our reputations and cause the Crasmeres to faint away with gasps of horror. Our transportation is more than sufficiently respectable and in their new coats, so are our coachmen. *Do* try to relax and enjoy yourself, my love.'

Lady Cecilia knew that she could be certain about two things regarding her husband. She was complacently confident that she could more often than not persuade Sir Joshua to come around to her point of view, knowing that his love for her was artlessly genuine and that he disliked denying her anything. However she also knew that on those occasions when he had made up his mind he was utterly immovable, and she had learned to accept these few defeats with a good grace as being the price of her far more numerous victories in more important matters.

The gardener and the stable lad had been given strict instructions to proceed at a sedate pace and the two carriages rolled pleasantly through the gates, leaving behind the crunch of gravel and the heady honey scent of the newly popular Euphorbia, a prized recent addition to English gardens originally from Madeira and the Canary Islands with which Ned had had considerable success.

Sir Joshua sat back and drank in the soothing green and blue of his familiar world all around him and gently and unselfconsciously held his wife's hand in a bid to calm her, and saw by the way she smiled at him affectionately that he had at least in some measure succeeded. In the landau behind them Kitty, Olivia and Alice had been discussing with some animation and anticipation how magnificent Wraxton Place might be and what artistic treasures might await them, but they too were eventually seduced by the beauty of the day and their conversation gradually petered out. It was only then that it struck Kitty that James had barely spoken a word and indeed seemed somewhere else entirely in spirit. She leaned forward and regarded him searchingly.

'Is all well with you?' she asked softly, the knowledge of what she had read in Dr Astley's office giving her words what was perhaps an unusual intensity. Her cousin slowly dragged himself out of his reverie and blinked at her as if waking up from sleep.

'Why yes, Kitty, I am quite well, thank you,' he said with apparent surprise. 'What makes you ask?'

'You seemed … er, *elsewhere* with your thoughts, I suppose, not present here with us. Forgive me if I was mistaken.'

His smile was so patently false that it took all her willpower to quell her unruly nature and swallow the sharp rebuke that leapt instinctively to the tip of her tongue. The need to understand what ailed him burned ever brighter in her, fuelled by the tantalizingly limited information from Dr Astley's file, but she could not think of any acceptable method to prise him open any more than she could open a recalcitrant oyster without a shucking knife. They continued for an hour or so before turning off the country road between massive stone pillars that were more like miniature bastions than gateposts, bearing glittering gates of extravagantly complex whorls of gilded wrought iron, and entered the grounds of Wraxton Manor.

Once through the discreet screen of trees obscuring the property from the outside world they entered a long drive as straight as a die lined with mature beech trees that marched along its considerable length with martial confidence and precision. The approach eventually gave out onto an enormous circular drive before a lofty pillared entrance that dwarfed the one James and Kitty had recently seen at Lionhurst, and would not have disgraced the entrance to the Pantheon in Rome. Copies (at least Kitty assumed they were copies, but with aristocrats as wealthy as the Crasmeres one could never be certain) of Greek and Roman statues were spaced at precisely equal intervals like ancient stone sentinels lining both the drive and the central island, which boasted an elaborate fountain in which muscular Herculean warriors bore aloft chubby cherubim holding jugs from which water poured with pleasing coolness, tinkling and sparkling in the sunshine.

Bewigged footmen in elaborately embroidered blue frock coats and yellow breeches hurried out to meet them and let down the carriages' steps and opened the doors. An unsmiling older man in an unrelievedly severe black velvet frock coat followed them and greeted the Stricklands with a perfectly executed bow as they emerged onto the driveway.

'Sir Joshua, Lady Cecilia, my name is Roberts, and I am Lord Crasmere's majordomo and butler. Please permit me to welcome you to Wraxton Place. If you and your family would be so good as to follow me, Lord Crasmere and his family are expecting you.'

They followed him up wide marble steps under columns that seemed impossibly tall through massive bronze–adorned doors into the hallway. The entrance hall was an enormous atrium filled with light filtering through a glass dome whose coloured panes painted the inlaid floor and indeed the visitors themselves in jewel–like colours. Niches with both male and female Greek and Roman statues, some of whom were shockingly bereft of all clothing, seemed to fill every nook and cranny. They trooped across the echoing space through a doorway that would have served perfectly well as the entrance to a modest Greek temple and entered a drawing room three or four times the size of the one at their home in Longton Manor.

Colourful classical and historical scenes floated

airily high above them in gilt–edged panels whilst below ornate sofas had been arranged around a low table. All the Crasmeres apart from Lady Georgina got to their feet and came forward to greet them.

'How delightful to see you all again,' said the Earl, with a polite nod of the head to Lady Cecilia and her husband before moving on to the others. He again inclined his head politely to James and the three women but to Kitty's consternation then took her hand and brushed it with his lips, looking deep into her eyes.

'But it is an *especial* delight to see *you*, my dear Miss Kitty.'

His eyes really were *very* blue and his jaw very square, she thought, and had to admit to herself that on balance while his forwardness was provocative it was also intriguing and not entirely unattractive. And he had that unconsciously confident air of someone used to being in charge and assuming they would be obeyed unquestioningly.

They seated themselves and Lady Georgina apologised for remaining seated, blaming her painful joints, irritably tapping her cane on the floor for emphasis.

'These damned pins of mine have become more unreliable than the promises of a Frenchman,' she said querulously, 'and I was fortunate indeed that they were on their best behaviour for the night of your ball!'

Roberts supervised two maids bearing large silver trays laden with teapots and jugs and sugar and cups and saucers and confectionery, in short all the paraphernalia of teatime. Once all had been laid out to his unsmiling satisfaction, he waved impatiently for them to begin the business of pouring and offering biscuits and tiny sandwiches, and only when they were done did he dismiss them with a jerk of the head and follow them out, bowing deeply and closing the drawing room doors behind him.

The Earl's younger brother and sister chatted animatedly with Olivia and Alice while the Earl and his mother conversed with Kitty and her parents. They spoke of the common and inconsequential topics deemed safe and uncontroversial by society and therefore much favoured on such semi–formal occasions, particularly between individuals only recently acquainted. Kitty mentioned their gardener's success with Euphorbia, a newcomer to their shores and the Earl leaned forward.

'We are fortunate enough here at Wraxton Manor to have what are, I believe, some of the finest gardens in the county, and, as the weather is fine and I see you have an interest in such matters, I would deem it a privilege to show you some of the highlights. Shall we?'

He got to his feet and she could think of no reason to demur. She took his proffered arm and let him lead her out of the drawing room and thence to the main entrance. A fraught hush gripped the sumptuous drawing room, broken only by the delicate clinking of cups upon saucers as those present sipped their tea and racked their brains for something to say in order to break the uneasy silence.

'*Well!*' said the Dowager Countess finally with a sigh. 'I must confess I am *more* than a little taken aback, but I regret to say I have long ago had to accept that my son does rather march to the beat of a different drum from most of us, irrespective what anyone else thinks. I am afraid he was the apple of my late husband's eye and I dare say he was too frequently allowed free reign where discipline was required. I would of course have accompanied them were I able, as there really should be a chaperone present, but as you know … ' she sat back and gestured resignedly at her legs.

Olivia volunteered her services and when she stood up to all their surprises James leapt to his feet as well.

'After an hour in a carriage I would heartily welcome the opportunity to stretch my legs, dear lady,' he said, 'so please do not concern yourself, I beg you! My cousin and I shall catch them up momentarily and all propriety will be satisfied, I assure you.'

She looked up at him as if seeing him for the first time and nodded slowly. 'I would be most obliged,' she said, 'but I beg you, sir, do be circumspect when you approach them. He does not take kindly to being, er, … how shall I put it … supervised.' James bowed respectfully and held out his arm to Olivia.

'Well!' said Lady Georgina again, and threw her hands up in the air, consigning the strange and improper behaviour of the younger generation to the winds and washing her hands of her son's eccentric behaviour before rejoining the general conversation, which was tentatively attempting to re–establish itself. James and Olivia took a moment to calm both Lady Georgina and Lady Cecilia who were both clearly and deeply mortified, so that by the time they had reached the marble steps outside there was no sign of Hugh and Kitty anywhere.

'*Damn* them! The Crasemeres must have dozens of

flunkeys all about the place but there is not a one to be seen! What say you Olivia, do we proceed to the left or to the right?'

They scanned the grounds and driveway this way and that but there was not a living soul to be seen anywhere or any sign to provide a clue as to their quarry's whereabouts. Their eyes met and in perfect unison James pointed to the left and Olivia to the right, causing James to laugh out loud most uncharacteristically.

'As the chances are precisely equal in either direction, I have no choice as a gentleman but to follow your instinct. Shall we?'

With a smile Olivia took the proffered arm and allowed herself to be helped down the steps. They turned to the right and soon reached the corner of the main building where they stopped and looked about. Formal French–style gardens spread out before them in fanciful and symmetrical curlicues and swirls of colour, interspersed with immaculately grassed paths winding artfully between them to allow visitors to admire and walk through the riotously colourful displays. There were tall hedges and topiary in the far distance being clipped by gardeners with long shears, but nowhere at all that two persons could have reached in the brief time that had elapsed where they would not be immediately visible to any spectator.

'It would seem my woman's instinct has led you astray, James, and I must apologise for the inadequacy of my feminine intuition' said Olivia, and his smiling acceptance with no trace of irritation made her realise for the first time that her feelings for him were not of the nature she had allowed herself to believe. Rather than the passion of a young woman for a personable young man she felt familial love, a liking and a fondness as for a brother, and was barely aware of allowing herself to be led back in the opposite direction from which they had come while she attempted to come to terms with this unexpected revelation.

They walked past the imposing entrance and when they reached the other corner of the building stopped again and surveyed what they could see. There were more gardens, this time with displays of roses and climbers smothering arched walkways and, unlike the other side, a long building with walls covered in flowering vines with a row of wide open glass doors.

'An Orangery!' said Olivia. 'They must be in there, there is no other place where we would not see them! Come, James.'

She walked towards the Orangery some two hundred yards distant, and as they drew closer the peaceful afternoon was rent by a scream, quickly muffled. They stopped in their tracks wide eyed and James began to run, his boots making a rapid tattoo of crunching gravel like the roll of a drum as Olivia gathered up her skirts and ran after him as best she could, hindered as she was by her voluminous skirts and dainty slippers.

# X

'IT IS VERY kind of you to take the time to show me your gardens, Lord Crasmere, very kind indeed. Are they really as fine as you intimated?'

'It's all a matter of refusing to settle for anything less than precisely what you want, whether it is proficient gardeners or an *objet d'art* or a beautiful woman,' he said and patted her hand with a wide smile that, it struck her for the first time, really displayed too many teeth, flawless though they might be, as if it was their display and not any genuine amusement or pleasure that was the expression's purpose.

'Yes,' he continued and waved his hand to encompass the intricate swirls and stands of flowers before them, 'anyone who works for me learns very quickly that I will settle for nothing less than perfection, and if it is not delivered to me as expected, the consequences will be … *decidedly* unpleasant. Concerning gardens generally, though, there is a ludicrous school of thought that tries to emulate the appearance of nature, can you imagine? Why emulate nature when nature, if you will forgive the jest, by its very *nature* is ... wild and uncontrollable. No, and even though I suspect some would deem it unpatriotic to say so, the Frenchies have the right idea on this one. Create something that nature never could! Make the plants and colours and shapes bow down to *our* mastery, *our* design, to *our* whim, that's the ticket, eh! But enough of such boring matters, allow me to show you the Orangery, it is Mama's pride and joy.'

She followed him across the gravel, casting a wistful glance at the inhuman perfection of the extensive flowerbeds as she allowed herself to be guided towards the Orangery. She had to admit it was undoubtedly a fine building, its whitewashed stone walls and terracotta tiles giving it an appropriately Mediterranean air. He led her inside through open glass doors and she clapped her hands at the orderly row of orange and lemon trees, their brightly coloured fruit like glowing decorations in the sunlit interior. They were planted in enormous evenly spaced pots with a mellow ochre glaze decorated with dragons and fantastical creatures writhing around them in relief.

'Chinese,' he said laconically as she ran her hands admiringly over their glazed surface. 'Devilishly expensive too, I can tell you, but they do look quite the thing here, don't you think? Come over here.'

He drew her further inside towards a trompe l'oeil painting that covered a central section of the far wall, depicting a fanciful classical landscape of columns and Greek temples and rows of cypress vanishing in perfect perspective towards hazy mountains in an idealised far distance. As she stood admiring it, lost in marvelling at the artist's consummate ability to deceive the eye, she was startled to feel Hugh's hand on her waist. Believing he was merely about to guide her in another direction she turned around and to her consternation he took both her hands in his.

'My dear Kitty,' he said and his voice was low and gruff as he looked deep into her eyes. 'I have wanted to do this from the moment I set eyes upon you.' Without warning he pulled her towards him until she was crushed against his body and before she could cry out or remonstrate his lips were hard upon hers and she smelled whisky and tobacco and her stomach turned over as he attempted to insinuate his tongue into her mouth.

With a strength she did not know she possessed she flung his hands away from her, twisted her head to one side and screamed *Nooooo* as loudly as she could.

'Shut up, you stupid little chit of a girl!' He hissed at her venomously and to her horror his engaging smile had metamorphosed into a feral snarl, distorted with an animal–like hunger. 'Just spread … ' he was suddenly jerked away, his hand clutching at her sleeve and ripping it as James hurled him to the ground, standing over him with clenched fists and so overcome with emotion that for a moment he was unable to get his words out. Olivia rushed over to a sobbing Kitty and held her close, stroking her hair and murmuring meaningless soothing phrases.

'*You!* By all the damn gods, it *was* you that day in Chittambore! I was uncertain before but I am utterly sure of it now!' shouted James, his face suffused with rage. 'Never again, you filthy, perverted swine! Never again! Get to your feet, you disgusting murderous piece of excrement!'

He pulled him roughly to his feet by his lapels and Hugh stood swaying with wide–eyed disbelief at what had just happened.

'You, you ... bloody *nobody!* How dare you ... ' he spluttered, 'who do you think ...' he staggered and winced as James slapped him forcefully and open–handed across the face, the sound of it shockingly loud in the Orangery.

'How dare *I?* Let us see if you are as brave facing a man as you are when assaulting and dishonouring a woman. My seconds will call upon you. Accept if you dare.'

Two passing gardeners had by then entered the Orangery in time to witness both James' challenge and Kitty's pitiable state. He and Olivia helped and supported her out of the building and stopped for a moment as James called over one of the men, who stood there shifting from foot to foot and clutching his cap, totally at a loss.

'You there, what is your name?' he asked.

'Jenkins, Sir,' the man replied.

'Well then Jenkins, pay attention and listen very carefully. Tell the stables to bring the visitor's carriages to the front entrance, fast as they can, mind. This lady needs to get home as quickly as possible. Tell them to summon Roberts and he is to inform the Earl's visitors that Mr James Strickland says we need to leave immediately. *Immediately*, at once, do you understand?'

'Yes, sir.' James pressed a coin into the man's hand and he tugged his forelock, put on his cap and set off for the stables at a run. James thought he had detected a glint of malicious satisfaction at the sight of his master rubbing his flaming cheek and seemingly in shock, and surmised that Hugo Crasmere was not popular with his employees.

By the time James and Olivia had supported Kitty back to the main entrance both the Strickland's conveyances were drawing up and James bundled her into the phaeton driven by Tom and sat beside her.

'Tell Ned to get the rest of them into the landau and make for Longton as quickly as possible.'

While Tom conveyed the instruction to Ned he glanced at the entrance where Lady Georgina and her two youngest children were holding onto each other uncertainly as they watched the rest of the Stricklands descend the steps. The whole scene played out in a highly charged silence and James spoke quickly to Olivia as she passed by.

'Just get them into the carriage and say Kitty is unwell,' he said. 'Waste no further time in elaborations or apologies.'

'Tom!' he said, turning to the lad watching the unfolding events with bewilderment from his raised seat, 'back to Longton as quick as you can, if you please. Do not wait for the others!'

Tom nodded, clicked his tongue, cracked his whip, and they lurched off with a spray of gravel.

Less than two hours later all the Stricklands were gathered in their drawing room, and so pre–occupied were they with the awful occurrences of the afternoon that not a one either noticed or remarked upon on how small and plain their rooms appeared by comparison with the extravagantly lofty equivalents at

Wraxton Place.

Kitty had just been brought downstairs by Olivia after changing into a light day gown with a shawl around her shoulders but still tremulous and wide-eyed with shock. James and Olivia sat on either side of her on a sofa and each took one of her hands.

'If there is any way at all that you can tell us exactly what happened, my dear, I beg you to do so and put us out of our misery,' said Sir Joshua. 'James and Olivia importuned us to wait until we were all together to spare you the ordeal of repeating and re-living … whatever it is that occurred. Are you sure you are sufficiently recovered?'

Olivia put a comforting arm around her and Kitty nodded with a wan attempt at a smile as she looked around at her family. Her father, uncharacteristically grave and overcome with concern for her. Lady Cecilia, unconsciously shredding her favourite paper fan and creating a sprinkling of what looked like multi-coloured snow around her feet, the powder on her face streaked with tears. Alice's face was in similar disarray, her hands covering her mouth and her normally coiffed blonde ringlets ravaged by the wind of their speedy return and almost unimaginably with no subsequent attempt made to repair the damage. And lastly James and Olivia flanking her as comforters and fierce guardians.

She seemed to draw strength from them all and slowly withdrew her hands from James and Olivia's gentle grasp. She leaned forward and her voice became stronger with every word as the desire to recount accurately what had happened and a mounting sense of outrage infused her.

'You all saw Lord Crasmere offer to show me the

gardens,' she began. 'I was so surprised I simply agreed – after all, I really *did* want to see the gardens, although in the event I quickly came to the conclusion that the French method does not appeal to me in the least. You know that I care little for many of the petty rules by which our society is regulated, and so we were already outside by the time I collected myself and realised I should have asked someone to accompany us. I said as much and he laughed and dismissed my concerns out of hand, saying we were now in *his* domain and that whatever he decided was acceptable, *was* acceptable. He had me firmly by the arm and it would have been not only extremely embarrassing but also physically difficult to forcibly extricate myself.'

'We had only been in the Orangery for a few moments and I was admiring the trompe l'oeil wall painting when he laid hands upon me, initially upon my waist. I simply did not understand what was happening until he spun me around very roughly, drew me to him and forcibly tried to kiss me. I cannot sufficiently convey to you the transformation in him, from superficial arrogant aristocrat to something more akin to a feral animal. When I struck away his hands with the strength of desperation I was truly afraid for my life and that was the moment when James pulled him off me and cast him to the ground, ripping my sleeve as that foul creature grasped it.'

Horror was writ large on the other three women's faces, while the expressions of the two men said more clearly than words ever could that if Hugh Crasmere had been present at that moment it was unlikely he would have left the room alive.

'I pulled him to his feet and could see that far

from being in any way repentant he was about to explode with outrage at being thwarted,' said James. 'I slapped him as hard as I could and said my seconds would call upon him and that is when I sent for the carriages and the rest of you.'

Kitty seemed to have regained some of her composure and indeed some colour had returned to her cheeks but upon hearing James' last statement the resurgent pink disappeared once more as she rounded upon him and gripped his arm, ashen–faced.

'*James!* Oh, James! You should not have done that! You have challenged him to a duel and he will be honour–bound to respond and he may kill you! I would not lose a night's sleep over that ghastly man's demise, but you! We have only just been given the chance to welcome you into our family and already it seems … oh I *beg* you, apologise! I know it will stick in your throat but I cannot … I mean *we* simply cannot lose you now!'

This was followed by a long silence broken only by Alice and Lady Cecilia's sniffling.

'I suppose there is no way out of this?' Sir Joshua said heavily. 'No way to avoid this madness?'

'I fear there is not, sir,' replied James. 'Even were I to apologise – which I am afraid I could not bring myself to do under any circumstances whatsoever – I feel certain he would not accept it, being too arrogant by far to contemplate the risk of being branded a coward. And now, finally having the full measure of the despicable creature I am dealing with I have no choice but to see this through. What occurred today, dreadful experience though it must have been for Kitty, is as nothing to the crimes this monster has already committed!'

He broke off abruptly and shut his mouth with an audible click, his expression betraying that he had inadvertently let slip far more than he had intended. Of all those present only Kitty was not surprised at his outburst due to what she had observed at the ball, as well as the tantalising information she had glimpsed at the doctor's surgery. All the rest of those present seemed nonplussed and looked at each other with bewilderment but James raised a hand to forestall them.

'Forgive me, there is more to this, much more, and I will tell you everything, I promise you. But only after this doleful business is done with. Grant me that time and do not question me further, I beg you.'

His manner brooked no opposition and there was little any of them could say after that. Kitty was driven to distraction by being so close to uncovering the secret that lay in James' past and yet being thwarted at the last hurdle. But all that was as nothing compared to her fears for his safety.

'What will happen now?' she asked with a catch in her voice. 'How will this insanity actually take place?'

'I gave Tom a note and sent him to Wallstock to summon Dr Astley and Mr Bagstock as soon as we had returned and I intend to ask them to act as my seconds. They should arrive shortly and will assist me with the details of the challenge and will then deliver it by word of mouth to my opponent's seconds, assuming he too has appointed a second or seconds, which I am certain he must have. I have heard previously that it is unwise to commit such matters to paper for legal reasons. The two groups of seconds will first and foremost endeavour to bring matters to a close without the necessity of a duel.'

He heaved a deep sigh and continued.

'Unfortunately there is no possibility of that endeavour succeeding as *I* do not wish any other outcome than to remove that evil creature from the face of the earth. Consequently the next matters to be decided will be the choice of weapons, the time, and the place.'

As if on cue the doorbell jangled loudly, making them all jump and Jackson showed in Dr Astley and Mr Bagstock, both with grave demeanours. They all knew Dr Astley and after muted greetings James introduced him to Mr Bagstock, as they had seen each other at the ball but not spoken to each other or been formally introduced.

'Dr Astley, allow me to introduce Mr Ernest Bagstock of Messrs Finch & Appleby. He has been extraordinarily helpful in my quest for a home, and I am happy to call him friend as well as valuing him in his professional capacity. And it was he who so artistically decorated our dance floor. '

Dr Astley shook his hand and murmured a word of praise for his artwork, but in light of the weighty matter at hand nodded to the rest of the family and James ushered the two men out of the room to the library. They were there for some time before James escorted them outside where they shook hands grimly before mounting their horses and riding off towards Wraxton Place.

It was dark by the time the sound of their horse's hooves on the gravel announced their return. They conferred briefly with James in the library before departing and he returned to the drawing room where the rest of the family awaited him expectantly.

'It is all arranged,' he said wearily. 'There is a

meadow a short ride from here that I believe is known locally as Oak Tree Meadow. It is accessible on foot and on horseback but is nonetheless well hidden from the road and has been agreed upon as a suitable place. We are to meet tomorrow morning at dawn, which I understand will occur at approximately a quarter past five. Crasmere's seconds are to be his brother Frederick and his majordomo, Roberts. The weapons of choice are pistols and he has agreed to provide them, a particularly fine matched set by Wogdon & Barton, according to both Ernest Bagstock and Dr Astley.'

'*No!*' The exclamation escaped Kitty involuntarily and she grasped his lapels and shook him as if he were a naughty child. 'No, James! This is archaic madness, do not throw your life away for the likes of Crasmere! I beg you! I entreat you!'

He looked down at her and disengaged her hands as gently as possible before looking around at all of them.

'I am the most fortunate of men,' he said quietly. 'I may have lost a dear parent but I have also gained the kindest, warmest and most welcoming family any man could possibly wish or hope for. And now that the fates have granted me the opportunity to right a wrong that has lain hidden and festering in my soul for years, my only regret is that should I fail I will have brought sorrow into this house, where I would only ever wish for happiness and sunlight to hold sway. I thank you all from the depths of my soul, and hope to see you all tomorrow for breakfast. Good night.'

He reluctantly released Kitty's hands before wishing them Good Night and retiring.

# XI

KITTY ATE NOTHING at dinner as the very thought of food made her feel ill. She lay in bed unable to sleep until exhaustion finally overtook her and it seemed that she had only just closed her eyes when her maid Lucy was shaking her gently and exhorting her to wake up. She was about to speak sharply to her for this unwarranted behaviour when the events of the previous day came flooding back and she remembered telling Lucy that if she failed to wake her up at four o'clock in the morning there would be dire consequences, too preoccupied to realise that it meant Lucy had to ask poor Tom to sit with her to keep each other awake and ensure they could wake her up at the appointed time and make her horse ready.

Kitty donned her riding dress and wrapped a dark cloak around herself before slipping out quietly by the kitchen door where Tom waited patiently with Bella, yawning and rubbing his eyes. She thanked him as he helped her up the mounting block steps and into the saddle but he retained his grip on the bridle with a furrowed brow.

'But Miss Kitty! You can't go out alone! Wait a moment and I will saddle Balthazar and accompany you!'

'Not today, Tom,' she said softly but determinedly. 'This is something I must needs do alone.' She clicked her tongue and before Tom could think what to do she and Bella had trotted away and disappeared into the darkness. A half moon appeared fitfully between drifting clouds and provided just sufficient light for her to navigate the country roads, which, fortunately, she knew like the back of her hand. She was also familiar with Oak Tree Meadow as she had ridden there before, and when she arrived she followed a muddy track to the group of ancient oaks that gave the meadow its name, imposingly sad remnants of the vast forests that had once covered the whole island. There were some thickets and a fence with a small gate behind them, through which she led Bella and tied her to a low bush that would allow her to graze.

She made her way back to the oaks, relying upon her instinct that the duel would take place nearby as it was the obvious landmark, and settled herself in deep shadow behind one of the largest trees, wrapping her cloak tighter around her and settling herself on the rough ground by the trunk to wait and battle to try and stay awake. She could not believe that with the horrors about to ensue sleep was still threatening to overwhelm her and was almost dozing when she became aware that the horizon had begun to lighten and the surrounding darkness slowly dissipated and drained away until there was enough light to see everything clearly.

Three mounted men arrived and she recognised the detestable Hugh Crasmere accompanied by his slim younger brother Frederick and the gloomily black–clad figure of Roberts, the majordomo. She got to her feet and stood behind the oak's massive trunk, her gloved hands resting on the rough bark as she watched them dismount. The two Crasmeres handed their reins to Roberts who led the horses to one side and tethered them to a nearby bush.

No sooner had he walked back to his masters than the thud of approaching hooves announced the arrival of James and his two seconds. Once they had dismounted and seen to their horses they approached the other group.

'Lord Crasmere,' said Dr Astley, his voice resonant with sincerity, 'can I really not prevail upon you to apologise and put an end to this unnecessary madness? I beg you, Sir, this sort of thing belongs in the past and has no place in current civilised society!'

Frederick Crasmere also opened his mouth to speak but Hugh cut them both off with an impatient gesture and a humourless bark of laughter.

'Gods, it is like being surrounded by a gaggle of old women! Apologise? If this untitled nobody gets down on his knees and begs for mercy I just might – possibly – be inclined to grant it! What say you, Strickland? Last chance to save your skin?'

James stepped forward and for a moment Kitty thought he might actually do so. But he simply drew off his gloves and threw them aside, turning to Roberts.

'The pistols, if you please, Roberts. Quick as you can, now.'

Hugh frowned at James ordering his man about, but nodded and the majordomo did as he was bidden, opening a voluminous saddlebag and returning with a gleaming brass–bound mahogany box. He opened it and held out its contents nestled in fitted velvet–lined recesses for inspection by Dr Astley and Mr Bagstock who each took a weapon and inspected it closely, exchanging them lest one notice some defect missed by the other. But after thoroughly checking the mechanisms and the charges they nodded grimly and replaced them in the velvet–lined box.

'Took bloody long enough,' said Hugh impatiently. 'Pick one, Strickland and let's get on with it.'

James did so, hefting it to get a feel for the weight and sighting down the barrel until he was satisfied.

'I congratulate you, Lord Crasmere,' he said. 'These are indeed extremely fine pistols! I wish I had had such with me when the Sergeant at Arms taught me how to shoot! But I believe I managed not to disgrace myself nonetheless.' He smiled a hard and unforgiving smile. 'I don't believe you have any military experience, have you, my Lord?"

Hugh remained tight lipped but did not rise to the barb and betrayed no other reaction.

'Gentlemen, take your positions!' said Dr Astley, who, it had been agreed, was to oversee the duel itself.

'By mutual agreement we will follow the French method. The combatants will stand back to back and upon my signal I will begin the count. The combatants will take one step forward for each count. Upon my uttering the word "Ten" they may turn and fire at will. The duel will cease at First Blood and the matter will then be at an end.'

Kitty felt her legs give way as the two men walked towards each other and James shook his head emphatically. 'First Blood will not do, Doctor Astley.

We will fight *à l'outrance*. To the death, for as long as it takes.'

All the seconds stepped forward to remonstrate but Hugh pointed his pistol at them with a wide and humourless grin that bared his teeth like a snarl.

'So the little nobody with no title wants to play a more serious game,' he said dismissively. 'So be it! *À l'outrance* it is, and I shall take great pleasure in watching him choke on his own blood and his grandiose gesture! Yes, yes, I agree to the new terms. Come on, come on, let's get on with it, I want my breakfast after I plant this clod in the dirt where he belongs. Doctor?'

The surgeon was pale but steady, being no stranger to death, but had no choice other than to follow the two combatant's instructions.

'Very well, if the two of you are each so determined to annihilate the other, regretfully I cannot stop you. Gentlemen? Take your positions.'

Kitty was clinging to the tree trunk for dear life and felt as if her legs might give way as the thought that one of these men was going to die in the next minutes became imminent and inescapable. Even the secret hope she had harboured that if James was shot his wound might not be fatal and he would recover, honour intact, had been dashed by his reckless folly and she was paralysed by her helplessness.

The two men stood back to back in shirtsleeves, pistols held to their chests pointing upwards, and the doctor began, his words like ominous drumbeats.

'One.'
'Two.'
'Three.'
'Four.'

'Five.'
'Six.'

The men each took a measured step forward away from each other in time with each number as it was uttered. As the word 'Six' rang across the field she saw Hugh hesitate and with bared teeth suddenly swing about to aim his pistol at James' retreating back.

'*Jaaaames!*' There was no time for anything other than his name but the raw terror and desperation in that one word was dredged up from some place deep in her soul and seemed impossibly loud.

Hugh was startled and his arm wavered as he fired while James spun around and dropped to one knee, simultaneously bringing up his pistol in one smooth motion and fired in turn, the two shots so close together they almost merged into one sound, deafening in the early morning stillness. Hugh was thrown backwards and lay spreadeagled on his back, a bright red stain spreading across his chest in shockingly vivid contrast to the snowy whiteness of his ruffled shirt. After one look to be certain that Hugh was indeed dead James rushed to Kitty and caught her as her legs finally gave way and tenderly sat her down against the oak's trunk.

'Oh Kitty, my dearest Kitty! You should not have been here to see this. But you undoubtedly saved my life, so I cannot but have conflicting emotions about it!'

He essayed a smile but felt a hand on his shoulder and looked up at Dr Astley.

'Come, James, make haste, we must leave this place with all possible speed! Frederick and Roberts must deal with Crasmere's body, but our side must on no account be seen with them! Swiftly now! I will accompany them and the body to Wraxton Manor, not as someone involved in a duel, but as a physician to agree with the family upon the cause of death to appear on the death certificate. These things are after all often treated as murder even though the courts are frequently sympathetic and often reduce such matters to manslaughter. I will come to Longton Manor as soon as I am able once that dismal business is concluded.'

---

It was not long past six o'clock when James, Kitty and Ernest Bagshaw rode up to the Strickland home and had their horses taken by Tom, whose demeanour brightened considerably when it became clear to him that nobody was going to berate him for allowing Miss Kitty to ride alone without a companion. The other staff were just commencing their chores for the day and were instructed to make coffee and lay out breakfast for everyone as quickly as possible. The family had already hastily assembled in some disarray, attired in various robes and gowns with their hair hastily brushed or not at all and it took some time for Lady Cecilia and Alice to regain their composure and dry their tears. Even Olivia, the most sensible and collected of them all, took some moments dabbing her eyes before collecting herself.

'My boy! My dear, dear boy!' said Sir Joshua, heaving a huge sigh of relief and hugging James in a most uncharacteristic display of emotion. 'Thank God you are unharmed! I cannot express how abjectly grateful and utterly relieved we all are to see you again, whole and in one piece. Look, Jackson is signalling that our hastily put together breakfast has been laid. Come, let us to table and you can tell us all about it.'

The three arrivals fell upon the bread, cheese and hams as if they had not eaten for months while those who had remained behind showed little appetite for anything other than coffee and the details of the duel, unable to conceal their mounting impatience.

It fell to Ernest to be the first to sit back from his repast and after a quick look at his companions decide to take up the story. That he, a virtual stranger, was willing and brave enough to do so raised him several notches in their general estimation.

He recounted the arrival of the two parties, the examination of the pistols, the switch of rules insisted upon by James, and when he got to the duel itself he glanced at Kitty, who by now had finished eating and was gratefully sipping her coffee. She nodded to him encouragingly and he continued, rather more hesitantly than before, his audience hanging eagerly on his every word.

'Nobody could have foreseen what happened next,' he said. 'Remember that we were all quite unaware that Miss Kitty had concealed herself behind the oaks. The two combatants were to take ten paces with their backs to each other and then turn upon the number ten being called and fire at will. I can still scarcely believe it, but it was upon the count of six that Lord Crasmere all at once stopped in his tracks, turned about and raised his pistol. There can be no doubt in any observer's mind that his cowardly and dastardly intent was to murderously and callously shoot James, er, Mr Strickland here, in the back. It was only Miss Kitty's cry, suffused with such desperate urgency and mortal fear, that had the dual effect of startling Lord Crasmere and warning James. The former's shot missed, and James' did not. The Earl is certainly dead, and we immediately rode back here as fast as we could.'

'Dr Astley accompanied the body and Lord Crasmere's seconds to Wraxton Place in his capacity as a surgeon and physician and will do his utmost to ensure that the matter is officially laid to rest with the deceased. It is to be hoped that his stature in the community and eminence in his profession will ensure that his word is accepted without question, although that, of course, is entirely dependant upon the agreement of the Crasmeres to this course of action.'

They moved to the Drawing Room and were endlessly discussing the events at Oak Grove and demanding more details when the doorbell jangled and they all looked at each other in surprise at having an unexpected caller at this early hour. Moments later Jackson announced Dr Astley and Mr Frederick Crasmere and ushered them into the room. While they were all agog to hear what the consequences of the duel might be, none of them could imagine any conceivable reason for the presence of the younger Crasmere given the current circumstances.

The family resemblance to his only just departed older brother was strong in his general features and colouring, but in a leaner, softer version, wrought with a finer palette.

'First and foremost,' began Dr Astley, 'I am extremely relieved to report that the Crasmere family is willing to agree to a death certificate that quotes the unfortunate accidental discharge of his own weapon as the cause of death, which will certainly lead to a coroner's verdict – should one be deemed to be necessary – of death by misadventure. However, their agreement is conditional upon being ratified by Frederick here, who, as I assume you all realise, is now the new Earl of Wallstock, upon his return to Wraxton Place. And that in turn is conditional upon him receiving a satisfactory response to the question he wishes to pose to you, James. I urge you most strongly to do your utmost to persuade him.'

Frederick was deathly pale and had eyes only for James. Sir Joshua got to his feet and quite deliberately stepped between them, blocking his nephew from Frederick's sight.

'You have my sincere condolences and deepest sympathy, young man, but I cannot fathom what on earth you expect to learn here that you do not already know. To put it bluntly, what is it that you want?'

'I will tell you Sir. To put it equally bluntly, I wish to know why he,' – he leaned to one side and pointed a shaking finger at James – 'refused the initially agreed upon First Blood, from which both parties at least had a chance to walk away with their lives, and why he adamantly insisted upon fighting *à l'outrance*, to the death. Why, Sir? *Why?*'

James rose to his feet and indicated a vacant chair. 'You are entitled to an answer, and I will give you one. I had promised my family an explanation as well, so I am relieved to have to relate this unpleasant tale but once.'

Frederick was taken aback, clearly having expected some sort of dismissal or platitudinous rejection and sat down. James waved to Jackson.

'Irrespective of the hour,' he said, 'with your permission, Sir Joshua, kindly bring us a decanter of brandy and glasses for all of us. What I have to say is neither pretty, nor short, and I believe we may well have need of it.'

# XII

ONCE THE BRANDY was served James leaned forward in his seat with a haunted, faraway look in his eyes, resting his elbows on his knees. Kitty recognised the look as the same one that had once prompted her to tell him he had gone away from the present.

'My family already knows some of this in outline, so please forgive a degree of repetition but there are others here who are unfamiliar with my past,' he began.

'As some of you may recall, when I first arrived Sir Joshua and I briefly mentioned that my parents died in a coach accident. I was taken in by my mother's sister and her husband, Sir Joshua's brother, who had no children of their own. But sadly she was not a strong woman and never recovered from her sister's death and soon afterwards followed her beloved sibling to the grave. Well, Alexander Strickland had worshipped her and was inconsolable, and even though I was still very young I believe we took great comfort in each other. Just at this time an opportunity arose to buy into the East India Company and as he could not bear to live amongst the things and places that served only to remind him of the family tragedies and of the great love he had lost, he sold up everything and went off to India as I was deemed old enough to travel. He managed to find a kindly young woman who wished to travel to Bombay to join her father – and, we all suspected – in hopes of finding a better husband than she could in these shores, there being a considerable shortage of British women of marriageable age in that part of the world.'

He saw that Frederick Crasmere was fidgeting and becoming increasingly impatient and addressed him directly.

'Have patience, I beg you, Lord Crasmere. I give you my solemn assurance that everything I am saying is germane to your question.'

'My stepfather proved to have a knack for business and trade and it was not long before he established his own trading house, named simply Strickland & Son. He steadily improved our fortunes and prospered and we lived in a spacious bungalow with servants, terraces and gardens, and these were the idyllic surroundings in which I grew up. It was just outside a thriving little town called Chittambore, ideally placed for trade near a confluence of rivers that allowed access both to Calcutta and other points on the Bay of Bengal.'

'There were a handful of other British and Europeans, some administrators and a small military contingent as it was a sleepy little town whose primary value was as a trading post. As you know, Sir Joshua, your brother was an educated man and wished the same for me, but after the death of his wife he had changed and remained withdrawn and somewhat unsociable for the rest of his life to the outside world, but not to me. He was – quite rightly – dissatisfied with the education provided by the nearby garrison school and engaged a tutor, a well–educated Parsee lady named Mrs Khambata, a widow whom I believe I have mentioned briefly before. She more than fulfilled my stepfather's expectations and gave me an excellent education, and while nothing could ever replace my mother, she came to be like a member of the family and we became very close over the years.'

'My stepfather took me into the business when I was fifteen or so and I did very well there, sufficiently so that within a year or two he made me a partner. I stayed in touch with Mrs Khambata, and informally built on my earlier studies in the evenings and on Sundays as I was always hungry for knowledge and she was delighted to have so eager a pupil to whom to impart it. And it was a relief to my stepfather to be relieved of the responsibility of being my companion and mentor outside of the office.'

'For God's sake, man!' exploded Frederick. 'I didn't ask for your damned life story and have no interest in it whatsoever! Get to the point if indeed you have one and answer my question!'

'I am almost there,' said James with a nod, 'and then you will understand everything, and why I have been telling you this, I assure you.'

'As I was saying, we still spent many hours a week together, and as I got older I became very interested in the natural sciences, of which she had an encyclopaedic knowledge. One day we had arranged to go for one of the many walks we took along the river to observe and discuss the local flora and fauna. On the day prior to this my father deemed it necessary for the sake of good relations with his fellow Englishmen to make a rare appearance at a musical evening being held at the residence of the Colonel commanding the troops who made up the local garrison, and it was there that I first laid eyes upon both your elder brothers, Frederick, both Charles the Earl at the time and Hugh, the next in line. I was introduced to both of them although unsurprisingly they took little notice of someone who to them was little more than a tradesman. They were apparently on some sort of tour of India and the Colonel was some manner of distant cousin only too eager to bathe in an Earl's reflected glory.'

Frederick's impatient frown disappeared and was replaced with frowning concentration upon what James was saying.

'Charles was clearly a quiet and sober man who drank and ate sparingly and danced only the obligatory minimum with the somewhat ungainly daughter of the Colonel. I regret to say that Hugh, by contrast, quickly became so drunk he could barely stand and behaved most inappropriately with two of the officer's wives and had to be forcibly escorted from the building. I had no expectation whatever of ever seeing either of them again, and thought little more about it.'

'The following day was a Sunday and I had agreed to meet Mrs Khambata late that afternoon to avoid the worst of the day's heat, following a long path that wound through the jungle and eventually led to the riverbank. Now that I can remember everything, I can still feel being swallowed up an enveloped by the humid, lush green forest that covered the higher ground we had to ascend before the land eventually sloped down to the riverbank on the other side. All the while my friend and teacher was pointing out interesting or unusual insects, flowers and plants, at the same time being careful to stick to the path and keep a weather eye out for snakes. In many ways it was like being in the Garden of Eden.'

He paused and ran his hands over his eyes, his fingers lingering on the peculiar scar on the side of his face.

'It was during these pleasant moments that the peace of the jungle was shattered by raised voices and angry shouting nearby and we made our way curiously towards the noise. There was a quality of such fury imbuing what I was hearing that it made me fear the worst, gripped by a sense of foreboding as we stumbled into a clearing next to a rocky ravine just in time to see – please prepare yourself, Frederick – your brother Hugh bring the heavy silver head of his cane down on Charles' head – yes that very one he carried with him all the time – with such force that I heard his skull smash and he dropped like a stone, dead in an instant.'

There was pin–drop silence in the Drawing Room and James attempted to calm his quickened breathing before he continued.

'So focused was he on his bloody deed that he was not immediately aware of us standing motionless in horror behind him, and without a moment's hesitation he used his boots to roll Charles' lifeless body over the edge of the ravine as if it were no more than a log and watched it plummet down to land on the rocks below with a sickening thud. He threw out his arms and turned his face to the heavens and we clearly heard him say, 'Behold the new Earl of Wallstock!' in a tone I can only describe as gleeful exaltation.'

'The scene and his words were so horrific and appalling that Mrs Khambata could not stifle a gasp of revulsion and he spun around, his face covered in gore and snarled at us like a wild animal. Without hesitation he ran at us and even though I attempted to defend myself I was clumsy with shock and he brushed my blows aside and used the heavy head of the cane on me just as he had done with his brother only moments before. I will never again forget those moments! The brief struggle and how the silver elephant's head glinted in the sunlight as it crashed into the side of my head, and everything went black.'

'Oh, James,' said Kitty and there were tears in her eyes. 'It is so awful and horrible! Oh, poor you! But how is it that you survived?'

He gratefully allowed her to hold his hands in hers and seemed to draw strength from her as he continued.

'I believe what saved my life is the fact that injuries to the head, even relatively minor ones, bleed copiously and that the large amount of blood pouring from my head made him think he had despatched me as he had just despatched poor Charles. I lost consciousness for a few moments and when I regained it could hear a woman's terrified scream that was abruptly cut off.'

'I cursed most dreadfully as I tried and failed to get to my feet, going out of my mind with concern for dear Mrs Khambata but the blow to my head was too severe and even now that my memories have finally surfaced again I still have no recollection of the time immediately thereafter, and doubt I ever will. I was eventually found lying on the path that led to our house and some homing instinct must have directed me to somehow drag myself there. I was oblivious to the world for several days in what the garrison doctor described as a 'coma,' and when I finally awoke and very gradually returned to normal I had no recollection whatsoever of anything that had happened, not even of making the arrangement with my teacher.'

'When they eventually deemed that I was strong enough to bear it they told me that Mrs Khambata had gone missing on the day I was found, and that the authorities surmised we had both been attacked and that they had abducted her and I had been left for dead. Her body eventually washed up downriver some time later, too far gone by that point to give any indication of how she had met her end.'

'And there you have it, Frederick. I regret to say your brother Hugh murdered your oldest brother Charles for no other reason than wanting the Earldom for himself, of that I have little doubt. He also murdered my dearest friend and very nearly succeeded in murdering me.'

James leaned towards Frederick and held back his hair from the side of his face.

'Can you see it, Frederick? Look closely at my scar and albeit vague, you will see the shape of an elephant's head. Your brother left his murderous mark on me, and I will carry it there for the rest of my life.'

The silence in the room was profound as his listeners absorbed the enormity of his tale. Frederick was deathly pale, his hand covering his mouth as he stared at James in horror.

'But … how is it that all this came to a head only yesterday, years later?' he said uncertainly.

'Coming so close to losing me rather knocked the stuffing out of my stepfather,' replied James. 'I was all he had left and coming so perilously close to losing me made him withdraw from life even more than he had already. I believe he simply ceased to wish to continue living, and that when the cholera came he simply embraced it and lay down to die. In the time since my injury I sometimes had tiny flashes of memory, the merest fragments, frustratingly insufficient to draw any coherent conclusions. And then came the ball here at Longton Manor and I saw Hugh for the first time and that triggered something, but I could not tell what, and the same applied to seeing that damnable cane with the silver elephant's head he had with him. Now *that* produced such a strong reaction that I sought out Dr Astley who has been attempting to help me.'

'It was only when I saw him brutally manhandling Kitty that it was as if a veil had been ripped away and in an instant I remembered everything. I am most awfully sorry, Frederick. None of this has anything to do with you nor is there anything you could or might have done. All that filled my mind was that I could not allow this – forgive me again – vile, despicable creature to live and especially I had to prevent him harming her in any way, as he clearly intended to. And his behaviour in the duel is the clearest demonstration there could possibly be of his morally defective character. He was perfectly prepared to shoot me in the back without compunction because he could not countenance not getting his way, no matter what the cost.'

'Once again I am so terribly sorry, my dear Frederick, or I suppose I should call you Lord Crasmere now. I know it must be extraordinarily hard to hear this coming from the man who killed your brother. But the truth is that he belonged on the gallows long ago and I did what seemed to me was the only way to stop him. And to give justice to your brother Charles and to my friend and mentor Mrs Khambata. And for myself, and for his assault on Kitty, for that matter. I hope you can find it in your heart to hear the truth in my words.'

Frederick got to his feet and had to grasp the back of his chair to steady himself. He passed a hand over his eyes and looked at James, wide–eyed.

'I do believe you, Mr Strickland. I do, and wish to God I did not. I have always known there was this mad, utterly egotistical side to Hugh, and that he deeply resented and never came to terms with being second and not first in line to the Earldom. And when we were young I know he committed acts of cruelty upon animals and then later on farm lads who dared not fight back.'

'So I had no illusions regarding his qualities and that is why, as well as judging you to be a man of fundamentally sober and morally upright character, I believe you. But as well as that man who stands before me and who under other circumstances I might well have come to call friend, I cannot help but see like some dread shadow inextricably linked and conjoined, that man who shot my brother. I hope you will understand that it is something that may take me some considerable time to come to terms with.'

With a formal bow and a deeply troubled expression he wordlessly took his leave and they listened to the sound of his horse's hooves diminish and disappear into the distance.

# XIII

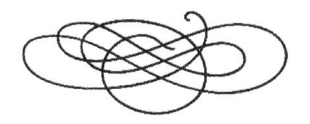

A TWELVEMONTH HAD passed since that desperate day that ended with the Earl of Wallstock's demise, an occurrence seldom mentioned in the county without appending the word untimely – or timely, depending upon whether you were one of the select group who were in possession of all the facts. To everyone's great relief Dr Astley's certified cause of death as being an accidental discharge of the Earl's own pistol had, as they had fervently hoped, been generally accepted without question or further comment, due in no small part to the physician's eminence and standing in the community.

It had been a year of changes and surprises in the family landscape of the Strickland family. James was a different man since his memories had returned and he had avenged both the murder of his dear friend and teacher and secondarily the murder of the then Earl of Wallstock, Charles Crasmere. Both these had liberated him and reborn him into his true nature that had hitherto been revealed only fitfully and in part. Having now largely cast off the shadows of the past that had been an oppressively deadening weight, allowed him to blossom and delight in conversing and amusing his family and acquaintances with his wit and erudition.

In the aftermath of the ball and the duel, Ernest Bagstock had proved to be a steadfast friend and companion to James, quite apart from rendering him immeasurable assistance in progressing his plans for Lionhurst. He was consequently a frequent visitor at Longton Manor, where, when not discussing property matters with James, he and Olivia were more and more frequently seen to take long walks and were often to be found discussing art and music, particularly so once she had seen and admired the many works he kept in his apartment, upon which excursions Kitty was only too happy to accompany them as chaperone and facilitate the burgeoning closeness between the two.

The heart–stopping desperation she had experienced when James' life hung in the balance on the day of the duel had finally forced her to abandon any thought of her plans to encourage Olivia and James to greater intimacy, which in truth had always been driven only by the concern for her sister's future absorbed from Lady Cecilia. She thereby freed herself from the cause of an unsettling and guilty inner conflict and gave herself up unreservedly to her feelings for her stepcousin, as she had come to refer to him. They were sitting in the peaceful and undisturbed tranquillity of her sewing room sanctuary, to which he had been hesitantly invited and which by some unspoken agreement had quickly become their preferred meeting place, when she finally confessed everything to him, unable to bear being in his presence while he remained ignorant of her attempts to deceive both him and Olivia.

He allowed her to pour out her confession without interruption and when she had finished leaned forward and brushed away the tear that had escaped her despite her best efforts to remain calm. She was in a ferment of fear that now, at the very moment when they were free to explore greater closeness, he would look at her with contempt after hearing what she had done and not wish to have anything more to do with her. He was still for a moment and smiled and took both of her hands in his.

'My dear, sweet Kitty,' he began, 'did you imagine that because of my memory loss I had lost all powers of observation and deduction? I could hardly spend the time here in Longton Manor that I have done without your mother's concerns for the future happiness and comfort of all three of her daughters, but especially her eldest, Olivia, becoming transparently obvious to me?'

'You occupied my thoughts from the very first moment I laid eyes upon you, and when after initially giving me some hope that my feelings were reciprocated, you seemed to blow hot and cold and inexplicably made the most unabashed efforts to conspire to place Olivia and myself in each other's paths, and I will confess I was initially somewhat confused. But when I realised what you were doing and more importantly *why* you were doing it, I simply did my best not to give Olivia any reason for false hope without being churlish or discourteous, in which endeavour I regret to say I may not have been entirely successful.'

'But I cannot make myself allow more time to go by without attempting to remove any last vestige of doubt or misunderstanding.'

To Kitty's astonishment he slid deliberately from his chair facing her until he was resting with one knee on the floor, and in her puzzlement her first thought was that it looked decidedly uncomfortable.

'Dearest, most precious and lovely Kitty,' he began, retaining his hold on her hands all the while, 'is it truly possible you do not yet know how I feel? Let me then be unequivocal and specific and avoid any ambiguity. I love you, Kitty. I know it is love because I have never felt such an overwhelming desire to spend every moment of the rest of my life with anyone before, not even remotely or in some lesser fashion. Let me say it again; I love you. And hope with every fibre of my being that you will consent to marry me, as soon as possible. What do you say?'

Kitty sat frozen in disbelief. While she had now allowed herself to hope that at *some* point she and James might become close enough for this to happen, for it to happen *now*, so quickly, had taken her breath away. She was even more astonished when he laughed outright.

'Oh, Kitty! You are a picture! May I take your open mouth as a yes?'

She had been quite unaware that she was gaping in a most unladylike manner and shut her mouth with an audible click that rattled her teeth. They had both risen to their feet and all at once were in each other's arms.

'Yes, James. Oh, yes! A thousand times yes!'

Lady Cecilia was somewhat taken aback as while her plans for James had indeed come to fruition, it had unexpectedly been with the wrong child, and the youngest one first, at that. Nonetheless, she told herself, despite the order being the reverse of her preference, a daughter married was a daughter married, and the family's estimation of James's wealth had risen considerably when they heard of his extensive (and expensive) plans for the restoration and improvement of Lionhurst. As Kitty was of age it was not strictly necessary for him to ask Sir Joshua for her hand in marriage, but he deemed it an indispensable courtesy in view of the warmth with which the family had welcomed him and in particular the kindness shown to him by Sir Joshua.

The two men remained ensconced in the Drawing Room for what seemed like an interminable amount of time to the impatiently waiting ladies of the house after Jackson had been summoned early in the proceedings and was seen to deliver a tray with a decanter of brandy and two glasses. When the two gentlemen eventually emerged the level of brandy in the decanter had lowered considerably, with a certain rosiness in the cheeks of the drinkers as a consequence. After all the congratulations and hugs and kisses and squeals of delight Sir Joshua announced thoughtfully that it might be wise to lie down comfortably to think about all the preparations the upcoming marriage would entail and made his way very deliberately up the stairs to his bedroom, from which he did not emerge until gently awoken for dinner.

Olivia was especially attentive to Kitty in her great happiness, and when they chanced to be alone looked her younger sister in the eye and shook her head in bewilderment.

'I could see all along that the two of you were attracted to each other,' she said softly, 'but I thought you must have decided there was something lacking in him in some way and that was why you made such efforts to convince me that James had feelings for me. And now it turns out that you not only had feelings but *love* each other! I could not be more happy for you, my dear Kitty, I do hope you never doubt that I truly mean that. But I must know, why did you do it? It was rather cruel, you know. He is an engaging and attractive man and for a brief moment I actually let myself believe that something might develop from our pleasant encounters but soon saw that amiability and friendship was all there was on his part, and had to accept that it was all it would ever be.'

Kitty tearfully explained what she had done and why she did it, and when she had finished Olivia relaxed with a sad smile.

'Done is done, Kitty, and I understand that – however misguidedly – you persuaded yourself that you were engaged upon a noble and selfless enterprise. I cannot comprehend how you were able to suppress your true feelings as you did, but can see that your motive was pure and that it was for your love of me, however ill–advised. Here. take my hand and let us agree never to speak of it again.'

After they had dried each other's tears and sat together in happy reconciliation for some moments talking about the imminent wedding, Kitty recovered sufficiently to fix Olivia with a sly and penetrating gaze.

'I believe we have spoken more than enough about me, dear sister, and now that my future course is set, the question is, what about you? It does seem that Mr Bagstock is a frequent visitor to our home, and I happen to have noticed that some of those visits are at times when, given their close consultations on so many of James' affairs, he must surely have been aware that James was away in London or upon some errand or other? I can only conclude that, knowing how you admire his artistic endeavours and in light of the fact that the two of you often seem utterly unaware of my presence when in each other's company, would I be wrong to think that there may well be some news in that respect in the not too distant future?'

Olivia blushed a bright crimson and Kitty clapped her hands in delight.

'I was certain of it! Oh Olivia, have you discussed it yet? Has he declared his feelings? And do you reciprocate them? Have you said yes? Tell me everything, I insist!'

It seemed that Ernest had asked Olivia to be his wife only a few days ago and had planned to speak to Sir Joshua in the near future as James had done, but when Kitty and James made their announcement Olivia and Earnest had agreed to hold back from proceeding, not wanting, as Ernest had apparently put it, "to steal their thunder."

'Stuff and nonsense!' Kitty exclaimed as they hugged each other and did a little jig of unrestrained happiness. 'These two things do not diminish each other, far from it, together they make them both a hundred times more wonderful! Oh, Olivia, I am so very, very happy for you! Come! We must tell Mama and Father! They will be ecstatic!'

---

'Oh, my darlings, I cannot tell you how happy I am!' exclaimed Lady Cecilia before hesitating and agitatedly fluttering her fan with a furrowed brow that was a clear indicator that she was thinking hard upon something that was at odds with her words. The fan was an expensive Japanese silk affair that was a gift from Sir Joshua, a replacement after he saw that she had absent–mindedly destroyed her previous favourite.

'What is it, Mama?' said Olivia anxiously. 'What could make you hesitate so? Mama!'

On their way down the sisters asked Jackson to winkle out their father from behind his Times in the Drawing Room, and ask him to attend the three of them in the library. At that moment Sir Joshua entered and stood stock still when Kitty ran up to him and clapped her hands with delight.

'Olivia and Mr Bagstock are to be married, Papa! Poor Ernest was planning to speak to you first but we were bursting to tell everyone and simply couldn't wait! Do you forgive us? Isn't it simply wonderful?'

He kissed his daughters and congratulated Olivia, but his eyes were upon his wife and her ambiguous expression.

'What marvellous news, eh, my love?' he said as he went to sit beside her, gently removing the fan from her nervous hands. It had been very costly and hard to find and seemed to be in imminent danger of suffering the fate of its predecessor.

'What is troubling you, my dear?' he said. 'Surely this news can bring nothing but happiness and joy? Please speak, beloved!'

His last words penetrated whatever was whirling around in her mind and she bit her lip, avoiding looking at Olivia's distress.

'Oh! Yes! It is good news, of course, that Olivia has found someone … of course it is! It is just that … oh, husband, I had hoped for someone from a family with standing and connections, you see! I am thinking only of her! Mr Bagstock is certainly *talented* – everyone remarked on the beautiful chalking of the ballroom floor, and it was extremely kind of him to leap into the breach at such short notice and upon such short acquaintance … *but* … he is merely a surveyor in a small country firm, my dear! Lives, I believe, in an apartment above a commercial establishment in the High Street! Is Olivia to move from Longton Manor and all this and her consequent status in the community,' – she waved vaguely around her – 'to an *apartment*? A few squalid *rented* rooms? No, no, my dear, the more I think about it the more unthinkable it becomes! It must not be!'

Unnoticed by all of them, fixated as they were upon Lady Cecilia's increasingly alarmed monologue, James had entered the room, having enquired from Jackson as to the family's whereabouts. When she ran dry and paused, he stepped forward and looked both her and Sir Joshua sternly in the eye

'Sir Joshua, please believe me that I mean no disrespect to Lady Cecilia when I say I am afraid I cannot stand by and allow such sentiments to go unchallenged. Ernest – Mr Bagstock – has become a close friend of mine, something of great value to me as I had no friends at all when I arrived here. A warm and welcoming family, yes, of course, but no *friends*. Ernest is not only highly intelligent, well–educated and artistically gifted but also the kindest, most obliging and hard–working of men. He may live in an apartment for the moment, but I can assure you that will not be for long. He and I are at this very moment designing a country house with a proper studio for him, a modest country house, it is true, but a nonetheless spacious and comfortable home. It is to be on a corner of the land belonging to Lionhurst, which I have sold to him for a nominal amount in recognition of the innumerable ways in which he has helped me. And I have assured him Lionhurst itself will always be open to him as if it were his own.'

'Regarding his income, which I understand will be of importance to both of you in order for you to rest easy in respect of Olivia's well–being, you should know that he is one of only two remaining partners in Messrs. Finch & Appleby and that the other is a gentleman of seventy–nine years and who is regretfully not in good health. Dr Astley has told me in confidence – and I do beg you all to respect that confidence and not allow this intelligence to leave this room – that the poor fellow has a weak heart and is not long for this world. He has no living relatives and has taken all necessary legal steps to ensure that the business in its entirety will pass to young Ernest. The business has thrived under Ernest's astute guidance, and he has plans to expand and open branch offices in other small cities. And finally, it is true he has no title, but then, neither do I, and you have welcomed me into your family and as your future son in law.'

All four Stricklands had been listening to his lengthy and impassioned speech with great attention and when he had finished Olivia rushed up to him and planted a kiss on his cheek while whispering *Thank You!* before retiring in confusion, blushing furiously. Sir Joshua turned to his wife and raised his eyebrows enquiringly.

'I do believe that should alleviate any concerns or doubts you may have harboured?' he said mildly, and she smiled up at him.

'It has, husband, it has. With such an eloquent advocate to whom we have entrusted one daughter, how could I stand in the way of the happiness of another? Come to your mother, Olivia and let me kiss you and congratulate you. And, husband? You may release my fan from safekeeping and return it to me, it will be quite safe now!'

***

James had ridden to town to apprise Ernest of the good news that his and Olivia's engagement was now official, and to invite him to dinner. Sir Joshua knew that this was one day when his cherished Times would have to take second place and remain at least partially unread, and soon forgot the closely typed columns he would normally have been studying so carefully and instead sat with his wife and oldest and youngest daughters as they all laughed and speculated and discussed wedding dates and wedding breakfasts and got enmeshed in the most improbable and outlandish suggestions thrown out in the exuberance of the moment. Soon after James had left they were joined by Alice and when the middle Strickland daughter heard Olivia's news she was characteristically excessively happy and excited and the one who came up with the most ridiculous suggestions, such as the whole family wearing blue and purple to match the Strickland coat of arms.

When the initial euphoria had settled down somewhat Lady Cecilia turned to Alice and squeezed her hand sympathetically.

'I do feel for you, my dear, but I know you will have no difficulty finding a husband if you set your mind to it. That is unless you have some news for us as well? The new Earl of Wallstock did seem rather taken with you! But I suppose that would be too much to ask for! Still, we must … '

Alice laughed out loud and shook her head, making her beautifully trained golden ringlets swing from side to side.

'Frederick *was* definitely interested, Mama, and in the beginning was both attentive and amusingly tongue-tied. And he was sweet in his own way, and quite handsome. But after the duel, even though he persisted, I could see that from then on he was unable to be with me in the way he had been before, unable to look at me without at the same time seeing the family of which the man who killed his brother was a member. And even though I believe that in his heart of hearts he could have overcome it, sadly his mind never could, and the ambiguity of his feelings was quite apparent as, to be frank, dissembling was not his strong suit. Don't look like that, Mama! He was so quiet and sweet and innocent – far too much so for me! I came to realise that he was not the one for me, I am afraid. How could I live with the hint of a veiled accusation always behind his eyes? There was nothing

I could do about it and that is that.'

'And do not spend too much time feeling sorry for Frederick,' she added, 'since taking over the reins of Wraxton Hall he has thrown himself into the task of running and improving it, and to his credit, also improving the lives of his servants and tenants. At our last meeting he seemed to have come alive and unfortunately it was all to do with his plans for Wraxton Hall and nothing to do with me! He was barely even aware of my presence!'

'What you may not know, however, is that his sister Lady Emelia and I have become firm friends – no, more than that, very close indeed. She had always intensely disliked her brother Hugo, and once she knew about everything that he had done, unlike Frederick, she simply put him out of her mind, dismissed his very existence and wished to have nothing to do with the whole affair. She even once said in passing that she thought he had received his "just deserts." Can you imagine, her own brother! Anyway, she feels the need to get away from the country which she finds deadly dull and spend more of her time at their London home, a mansion in Regent's Park. And she is begging me to go with her! Imagine! You will permit it, will you not? Mama? Papa?'

She saw the doubtful looks on both their faces and played her two trump cards.

'Mama! Papa! It will all be terribly proper and above board as the Dowager Countess will accompany us. She has been hit hard by Hugo's passing and the ensuing revelations and desires some distraction and to re-enter society and see friends and so on.'

She paused for dramatic effect and knelt before her mother, taking her hands in hers and gazing earnestly into her eyes.

'And the other thing to consider, Mama, is that through the Crasmeres I will have an entrée into the very highest circles of society! The ton! Emilia is even on friendly terms with two of Queen Charlotte's daughters, can you imagine! And I might even be included in balls attended by the Royal Family! Oh, Mama, this is an opportunity that comes but once in a lifetime! I must go! I simply *must!*'

She got to her feet slowly and uncertainly, taken aback by her mother's immobility and lack of response. One consequence of her flighty nature was that of all those present she was the least well versed in reading the nuances of her mother's expressions, but Kitty and Sir Joshua knew exactly what was going on in Lady Cecilia's mind and exchanged knowing glances.

Lady Cecilia, already happily relieved of two thirds of her life's most weighty burdens had just had her hopes of an Earl for Alice cruelly dashed, and only moments later had been presented with another vista of possible glittering futures unfold before her like some gorgeously precious and expensive map designed just for her daughter. She saw it all – the Palladian town house in Regent's Park, the splendour of lavish balls and soirées where Alice would mingle with the whole gamut of top society. For a fleeting moment she even dreamed of Alice meeting one of the Royal princes ... but there even her fertile imagination was unable to sufficiently nudge probable reality out of the way.

'Of *course* you must go, my darling girl, if that is

what you wish to do. Is that not so, Sir Joshua?'

Her husband had been about to marshal a series of cogent arguments as to why Alice should go to London, in the expectation of his wife's disapproval, but saw very swiftly that he had quite misjudged the situation.

'Quite so, my treasure, naturally she must go, I am as always in complete agreement with you. I am sure she will have many wonderful adventures with which to regale us if and when she can bear to tear herself away from the many delights of London society and visit her family in the boringly sedate countryside,' he said and mentally made a note to revise his opinion of his middle daughter, whom he would not have thought capable of such a masterstroke.

James and Ernest arrived only moments before Jackson sounded the dinner gong and Sir Joshua and Lady Cecilia led their daughters out into the entrance hall where the two men joined them. The older couple turned and looked back at Kitty and Olivia on the arms of James and Ernest, and Alice, her cheeks pink with excitement at the prospect of the many wonders of London waiting for her like an unopened box of precious jewels, and they two of them smiled at each without needing to say the words they were both thinking.

*We have done well, my love.*

# XIV

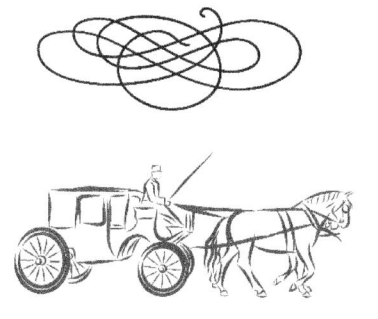

After breakfast upon the following day the Stricklands assembled on the driveway where Tom waited with the landau, resplendent in his new livery. Even though there was only to be one passenger, the interior was piled high with all manner of cases and boxes, so that Tom privately thought it was a blessing that Miss Alice was slight and slim as she might otherwise have encountered considerable difficulty squeezing herself into the remaining space.

Alice was looking her best in a new cloak in a flattering shade of burgundy with a pale fur trim and a dainty matching bonnet. She hugged her father, mother, sisters and James in turn before settling herself into the overburdened interior of the landau and kept waving as Tom clicked his tongue and the carriage lurched into motion. She pressed her face to the glass window to keep them in view for as long as possible and watched them dab at their eyes and reluctantly turn away before she realised that she too had tears materialising and hastily dabbed at them with a handkerchief lest they mark her powdered face.

A sad silence filled Longton Manor as the family went about their business, avoiding each other's eyes and suppressing the normal day-to-day banter that usually enlivened their domesticity. By mid-afternoon they had all drifted into the Drawing Room, where Sir Joshua resigned himself to the inevitable and lowered his Times with a sigh.

'When do you think they left Wraxton Place for London?' Lady Cecilia asked rhetorically, a question that was received in silence as none present could possibly know as Alice had not imparted any details about her departure other than the day.

'We do not know, my love, but what is certain is that as they did not depart at the crack of dawn they will have to overnight somewhere, and given who the Crasmeres are, I am sure Lady Emilia will have chosen only the most salubrious of establishments, or perhaps she has friends en route with whom they may stay, so do not fret, my angel, one way or another they will travel in the best manner possible.'

'Thank you, my love,' Lady Cecilia said gratefully, hitting her husband affectionately on the arm with her fan.

'You do know so well how to soothe me and you have indeed allayed my concerns for the journey. But, husband, *but*! She is so young still, so inexperienced of the outside world with all its wickedness, so what of the temptations of London! Have we done the right thing? Have we?'

Sir Joshua was exerting himself to formulate a pacifying response when Jackson appeared, looking uncharacteristically flustered.

'Begging your pardon, Sir, my Lady, but the landau is returning as we speak and … ' he paused, seemingly at a loss for words.

'And what, man, speak up!' said Sir Joshua, a little more acerbically than was his wont. 'Has a cat got your tongue?'

'It seems that Miss Alice has returned,' said the butler, stiffening at the unaccustomed reprimand. 'And … it seems she is accompanied in the landau by some other person, by whom I could not say.'

They looked at each other in mystification and as one moved to the Drawing Room windows in time to see Alice alighting, assisted by Frederick, the newly minted Earl of Wallstock. Alice took his arm and the pair made for the front door and disappeared from view. None of them had noticed Jackson's exit but he now reappeared, cleared his throat and announced the Earl of Wallstock and, with unusual formality, Miss Alice.

The pair entered the room and Frederick, gave a little bow and approached Sir Joshua.

'I have returned with your daughter Alice, Sir, as you can see, and realise that you expected her to be on her way to London by now with my sister. However Emilia completely neglected to inform me of her plans to take my mother, herself and Miss Alice to London, and it was only when my mother drove the servants to distraction as to what to take to our house in Regent's Park that I became aware of the plan.'

'I have to tell you that last night was a sleepless night for me as I imagined myself alone at Wraxton Place and while the absence of my mother and my sister would naturally cause me some regret, it was the thought of Alice being far away in London that gave me most pause. And when she arrived today … '

'He was practically *running* when he came out to meet the carriage at Wraxton Hall,' said Alice, glancing at him with an affectionate smile. 'Unsurprisingly Emilia was of course nowhere near ready for our departure, and after we had entered the house I saw the poor Dowager Countess sitting disconsolately amidst an amount of baggage that dwarfed my few poor boxes! And to my surprise Frederick drew me into their magnificent library – oh, Kitty and Olivia, you will both adore it! – and sat me down on a sofa.

'*You must not go to London!* he burst out and as you may imagine I was extremely puzzled and taken aback. And then … oh, Mama, Papa, Frederick has asked me to be his wife! Please be happy for me!'

'My apologies Sir, I had wanted to ask your permission first, but it seems I have been pre-empted,' said Frederick, looking somewhat abashed but at the same time adoringly at the object of his affections. 'I do hope we have your approval?'

'If that is what my lovely girl wants, how could I withhold my approval,' said Sir Joshua, vigorously shaking Frederick's hand and only desisting when he realised he had made the Earl of Wallstock wince by dint of his overenthusiastic grip.

Lady Cecilia had been transported to an inner circle of heaven by the news that although one daughter had *not* become the Countess of Wallstock due to the unfortunate demise of her planned partner, now all at once here was another daughter who *would* fulfil her ambition to have given birth to a countess.

She flew at the startled couple and put her arms around them both uttering cries of delight and congratulations, unable to fully grasp the enormity of her – and Alice's – good fortune, and Kitty and Olivia joined them in hugs and congratulations. Only James stood to one side, somewhat at a loss, and Frederick detached himself with some difficulty from the others and approached him.

'James,' he said hesitantly. 'Will you … ' James smiled and shook his hand firmly. 'My dear fellow, my heartiest congratulations. I have very recently come to count myself the happiest man in the world when Kitty agreed to become my wife, and I could not be more delighted to see you finding the same happiness with her sister. It is my sincerest hope that we will be as one family and put the past behind us.'

Frederick became serious at this reminder of the recent loss of his brother, but he squared his shoulders and looked James directly in the eyes.

'I have had some time to think long and hard about everything that happened, and the hideous acts that Hugo committed, and his utter lack of morality and concern for others. It is hard to face these things about one's older brother. Too many years separated me from Charles, who was always somewhat aloof and not given to expressing his emotions, so I looked up to Hugo when I was growing up, and did not allow myself to see the cruel and selfish side of his nature until I was much older, and even then tried to find excuses for his behaviour.'

'But now … I have had to face the unpalatable truth of what he was, and I cannot hold against you what you did after the suffering he inflicted upon you, and Miss Kitty. I believe I will be able to regard you as the honourable man you are and put the horrors of the past where they belong, namely behind us.'

He held out his hand again and they shook once more, but this time it was with a sincere determination to move forward to the possibility of a real friendship in the future. Jackson appeared once again and announced Mr Ernest Bagshaw, who was immediately assaulted by Lady Cecilia and her daughters to make him *au courant* with the most recent family development, which took some time as they all insisted upon speaking at the same time.

After heartily congratulating the couple he stood holding Olivia's hand, and was particularly gratified to see that the understandable tension between Frederick and James, whom he now regarded as his closest male friend, seemed to have been replaced by a mutual understanding and desire to be one family in the true sense of the word.

Jackson and Mrs Thrupp stood outside the Drawing Room, observing the scene before them. Lady Cecilia fanning herself furiously in a paroxysm of happiness hanging onto Sir Joshua's arm, whose face was wreathed in smiles as a consequence of his beloved wife's euphoria. The three young women each unconsciously emulating their mother and holding onto their intended's arms. And the three men, sharing the bemused and foolish smiles of the recently in love.

Jackson and Mrs Thrupp turned to each other with a most uncharacteristic smile on each face that would have engendered astonishment in any of the family, and, so strongly charged was the atmosphere with the headiness of romance and love, young and old, that for the briefest of moments the butler and the housekeeper held each other's gaze with some intensity before Mrs Thrupp shook herself like a dog shedding water and hurried away. Jackson watched her go with a speculative smile before returning to his usual expressionless demeanour as he closed the Drawing Room doors on the happy scene within and seated himself on a nearby chair to await the request to bring celebratory champagne that his experience told him would certainly be forthcoming at any moment.

## THE END

# Dramatis Personae

**Alexander Strickland** – Sir Joshua's late brother
**Alice Strickland** – Middle Strickland daughter
**Balthazar and Bella** – Strickland horses
**Charles Crasmere** – Oldest Crasmere brother, deceased
**Crauford's Light Brigade** – Major Harris' regiment at Almeida
**Dr David Astley** – Society physician and gentleman
**Ernest Bagstock** – Surveyor and partner in Finch & Appleby, engaged by James
**Georgiana Crasmere** – Dowager Countess of Wallstock
**Hugo Crasmere** – The current Earl of Wallstock
**Jackson** – The butler at Longton Manor
**James Strickland** – Alexander's sister–in–law's son, taken in by him after his parents died
**Jenkins** – A gardener at Wraxton Place
**Kitty Strickland** – The youngest Strickland daughter`
**Lady Cecilia Strickland** – Sir Joshua's wife.
**Lady Emilia Crasmere** – Sister to the late Charles Crasmere and his younger brothers, Hugo and Frederick
**Lady Tremayne** – Widow, close neighbour
**Lucy** – A maid at Longton Manor
**Major Harris** – The late owner of Lionhurst
**Mary** – Dr Astley's maid
**Mrs Khambata** – James' Parsee tutor in India
**Ned** – The gardener at Longton Manor
**Olivia Strickland** – The oldest Strickland daughter
**Roberts** – The Crasmere family's butler and majordomo
**Sir Joshua Strickland Bart.**– Head of the family
**The Hon Frederick Crasmere** – Third and youngest Crasmere brother
**Tom** – Stable boy and Ned's assistant at Longton Manor
**Mrs Thrupp** – The Strickland's housekeeper
**Mrs Upton** – A patient of Dr Astley

## Places & Things

**Almeida** – Seige in 1810 in eastern Portugal during the Peninsular War
**Bartletts' Tea Rooms** – Tea Rooms in Wallstock
**Chittambore** – A trading outpost in India
**Hillman's** – A bookshop in Wallstock
**Lionhurst** – A property James wishes to buy
**Longton Manor** – The Strickland family seat
**Messrs Finch & Appleby** – A firm of surveyors and auctioneers in Wallstock
**Oak Tree Meadow** – As the name suggests
**The Earl In Sunne** – An ancient pub in Wallstock
**Wallstock** – The local market town
**Whittaker's Emporium** – A fashionable shop in Wallstock, including women's fashions, whose proprietor is **Augustus Whittaker**
**Wraxton Place** – A very substantial property, family seat of Hugo Crasmere, Earl of Wallstock.
**Zastrozzi** – A new novel purchased by Kitty, published under the initials P.B.S, in fact Percy Bysshe Shelley.

# About the author

Michael Anderson was born, brought up and lived in Bombay (now Mumbai) in India. He left aged 18 and after a year at the University of Göttingen in Germany settled in London, where he has lived ever since.

He has a degree in Medieval History from the University of London and has had a variety of jobs, including Bollywood movie extra (as a teenager, unknown to his long–suffering parents), forklift truck driver (as an impecunious student) and freelance accountant. His passions are writing, history, and music.

Apart from writing, he has composed classical music and plays jazz bass with friends whenever the opportunity arises.

*Recollection and Retribution* is his sixth novel. His successful novel *Heaven's Above,* originally published by Jaico in India, now has a sequel entitled *Heaven's Above Three Years On.* His other novels are *The Return Of Magic, Not Where But When, Section O* and *Old Gods.* He has also written four collections of short stories; *Gardening By Moonlight, Nighthawks, Twelve,* and *Live Long And Prosper,* as well as a collection of poems in German entitled *Aus Meinen Fingern Gesogen*, all available on Amazon. For links to the books visit Michael's website or hover your device's camera over the QR Code.

### www.michaelanderson.org

# Books by Michael Anderson

1st short story collection

2nd short story collection

Novel set in a Bombay apartment building

3rd short story collection

Decorative collection of original German poetry

An epic fantasy novel.

A novel of war and time travel

4th short story collection

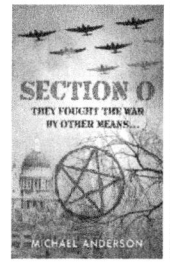

Novel of WWII and magic

Novel of time travel and ancient Britain

Sequel novel to Heaven's Above

Novel in the style of Jane Austen

Printed in Great Britain
by Amazon